Praise for the
Award Winning

THE ALIEN SKILL SERIES

Reviews:

"Most intense ending yet!"

"This series will be around for years."

"Wouldn't I just love to have the skill!"

"I'm hooked on Ben Archer."

*"I loved it! Every bit of it! Awesome
characters, awesome story, awesome plot,
awesome adventure!"*

BOOKS BY RAE KNIGHTLY

Prequel
The Great War of the Kins
www.raeknightly.com

THE ALIEN SKILL SERIES

Ben Archer and the Cosmic Fall (Book 1)
www.amazon.com/dp/1989605192

Ben Archer and the Alien Skill (Book 2)
www.amazon.com/dp/1989605095

Ben Archer and the Moon Paradox (Book 3)
www.amazon.com/dp/1989605141

Ben Archer and the World Beyond (Book 4)
www.amazon.com/dp/1989605044

Ben Archer and the Star Rider (Book 5)
www.amazon.com/dp/1989605176

Ben Archer and the Toreq Son, Book 6
www.amazon.com/dp/B08HWQYPH5

BEN
ARCHER
and

THE STAR RIDER

The Realm of Sand.

Rae Knightly

For information, go to:

www.raeknightly.com

Cover design by PINTADO
Book Formatting by Derek Murphy @Creativindie
Published by PoCo Publishers
ISBN Paperback: 978-1-989605-17-2

First Edition: September 2020

For Norma,
who came to our aid when we needed it.

CONTENTS

CHAPTER 1 *The Animal Whisperer*

The half-open briefcase revealed row upon row of stacked dollar bills, ready for use.

The man on the white leather sofa showed no interest in it, however. His eyes were glued to a TV screen placed on a white stand. He pressed the buttons on his handheld gaming control, watching intently as his avatar got slammed from all sides by the enemy. His concentration did not waver, even when a servant slipped into the room and stood by his side.

The servant with a clipped, dark-brown beard, whispered something into the man's ear, then waited patiently beside him.

The man's fingers froze on the gaming control, the game forgotten, while his avatar got trampled under the words: **GAME OVER**.

He leaned back into the sofa, rubbing his smooth chin, before picking up a different remote control and pressing the play button.

"Thank you! Thank you!" A woman appeared on another TV screen and grinned at the audience. She sat in a plush armchair on the set of a television program called *Charlie's Chit-Chat Show*, the name of which was sprawled on a glittery background.

"I'm so glad you're here to welcome a special guest tonight. He's a young boy who comes to us from Canada and who recently made headlines when he was photographed in a rather unusual setting. But let's ask him to tell us his story. Please welcome, Benjamin Archer!"

Applause followed, as a boy entered the scene and sat opposite the blond host. His brown eyes matched the colour of his hair and side fringe, which was combed to the side, though, unfortunately, it seemed the show's makeup artist hadn't had time to tame a rebellious mesh which stuck out from the back of his head. He wore jeans and a navy-blue shirt under a dark grey hoodie that was unzipped at the front.

The show host crossed her slim legs. "Hello, Benjamin. Thank you for coming out here from your native town of Chilliwack on the West Coast of Canada."

The boy cleared his throat. "Um, thanks. And, um, people just call me Ben."

"Right you are, Ben. Many of us have seen the stunning pictures taken of you by the famous reporter Jeremy Michaels from the Canadian Provincial Times. But for those who don't know what I'm talking about, let's take a look."

The glittery screen disappeared behind her and turned into an image of the ocean, the waters of which crawled with the most unusual gathering of sea creatures, ranging from whales, to orcas, to manta rays. Several similar images scrolled before the audience, who let out exclamations of wonder, not only because they were so spectacular, but because, in the midst of each one, Ben Archer bobbed in the water.

"Isn't that amazing?" Charlie gasped. "Benjamin... Ben. I think I voice everyone's question when I say: What on Earth are you doing in those pictures?"

A ripple of laughter flowed through the audience.

"Um... it's a gathering of animals that live in the ocean. They come together like this, once every couple of years, but it had never been recorded before."

"But you're in the middle of it all! Weren't you terrified?"

"I was, at first, until I understood what the animals wanted of me."

Charlie grimaced. "Ah, yes. These images are astounding in themselves, but it seems there's more to it than that. You claim that you can actually talk to these animals. Some people are even calling you an 'animal whisperer'. Why don't you tell us about that?"

The boy shuffled in his seat. "An animal whisperer? Yeah, I guess you could say that. It happened about a year ago. I started hearing my dog's thoughts..."—his voice faltered—"...then other animals started talking to me, like crows, whales, bees... They all told me the same thing. They are sick. And we're making them sick. It's not just that we're destroying their habitat and causing their numbers to dwindle, it's that more and more are showing signs of illness that will spread like wildfire if we don't do something soo..."

"Wait a minute, wait a minute!" Charlie interrupted. "Go back a bit. You said 'other animals started talking to me'. Do you realize what you are saying?"

The audience laughed a little too hard.

The boy blinked at her, a touch of annoyance creeping into his face. "Yes, that's what I said. Animals speak to me, and I can speak to them. I have offered myself as a translator between humans and animals, and they have accepted."

The host waved her hand at him as if he were going way off track. "Ben, hold it a minute. You do understand that claiming to be an animal whisperer is a little hard to swallow for us folks here. Tell me, how old are you?"

"Thirteen. Almost fourteen," the boy said.

"Okay, now listen. Before you say anything else, you will agree that we need to see some kind of proof of this superpower of yours. It's one thing to see these incredible pictures, but I thought we could do a little test, right here, in the studio. What do you think?"

The crowd whistled and cheered.

The boy tensed. "What kind of test?"

Charlie laughed. "Oh, nothing serious, I promise."

As she spoke, a spotlight came on and illuminated the right side of the stage, which was separated from the center by a curtain that dropped down from the studio ceiling. A man came into the spotlight, rolling in a small table with a cage on it. A white cat stared out of its bars.

"Ooh!" the audience cooed.

Charlie grinned. "Ben, we have a real, live animal behind that curtain..."

"You mean the cat?" Ben interrupted, his face slightly flushed.

"Wow!" the audience laughed, with sporadic clapping as some hadn't quite caught what had just happened.

"Yes, well done!" Charlie grinned at the audience. "I promise, this is all happening live. Ben didn't know about this."

Excitement built as another animal was brought on stage.

Charlie waved her hand at the crowd. "Don't say anything! Let's give Ben a chance."

The boy's slumped face indicated he was no longer enjoying the show, but he had to go along with it. He correctly guessed the tortoise, followed by the bunny and then the snake.

The audience buzzed while Charlie giggled. "How fun!"

"Yes," the boy said without conviction. "And now I need to tell you how we are endangering the lives of..."

"Oh, hold on a second, Ben. We only have a

couple more minutes. This is the last one."

The audience, hyped up by the game and eager to see more, cheered as a beautiful, brown horse was brought on stage. Its ears flicked back and forth on its head.

"Come on, Ben, we're counting on you," Charlie beamed as if she could see the number of viewers watching her show going off the charts.

This time the boy stood, a look of worry on his face. "You should get that horse off the stage," he said.

Loud applause.

The horse pawed at the ground and pulled at its bridle, giving its handler a hard time as he tried to keep it in tow.

Charlie clapped her hands in delight.

"No, really," Ben warned. "The horse is scared. She can smell the presence of the snake."

He had barely spoken when the animal reared, knocking over its handler. It crashed through the curtain into the glaring spotlights, neighing with fear.

Charlie shrieked and fell off her armchair.

Ben jumped in front of her, placing himself between the host and the terrified horse. Lifting his hands high, he stood his ground before the animal, which shook its mane to-and-fro and let out a shrill whinny.

The boy didn't move an inch, while Charlie held her hand to her heart, mouth agape and eyes almost popping out of her head.

The brown mare pawed at the ground, its skin gleaming in sweat as it snuffed loudly through its nostrils.

The audience watched, aghast, as the boy presented his hands to the horse, palms outstretched. The animal backed up a step, body trembling, ears flat. Then it approached the boy, gave a kind of bow and rested its snout in the boy's hand.

The boy's tense body relaxed. He approached the horse and began rubbing its neck, talking to it in a soothing voice...

The man on the white leather sofa pressed the pause button, freezing the screen on the boy and the horse. He glanced at the money-filled briefcase, deep in thought. Then with the smallest gesture of his hand, the servant sprang into action, locked the lid of the briefcase and hurried down a gloomy corridor to a back entrance.

Two heavy-set men in business suits waited in the glaring sunlight.

The servant handed the briefcase to one of them and said in broken English, "You get other half after it is done."

The one holding the briefcase glanced at his partner through black sunglasses.

The servant straightened, his face reddening. "You have Master's instructions," he insisted. "He wants the boy."

CHAPTER 2 *A Cloak*

Ben Archer dangled his legs over a rocky ledge. The first rays of the morning sun peeked over the horizon, warming his cheeks. He shielded his eyes, squinting at the lonely lake snuggled in the folds of the mountain.

He took off his parka as the sunlight chased away the morning chill. It had rained during the night, and the back of his jeans had become damp from sitting too long. Standing, he brushed off some dirt that stuck to his pants, never taking his eyes off the calm water.

Where is *he?*

Ben puffed his cheeks as he scanned the surface.

As if in answer, a mysterious blue glow

appeared in the depths of the pristine mountain lake.

Ben caught his breath. He snatched up his backpack and clambered down to the water's edge as the glow floated upward towards him. Bubbles broke the surface, releasing a sudden spray of icy water on him.

"Hey!" he protested, jumping back and landing in mud.

A man's head popped out of the water.

"Jeez' Mesmo, these are brand-new," Ben complained, shaking his black sneakers to get some of the mud off.

His alien friend grinned. "They won't be brand new once we're done with the day," he said as he stepped out of the lake, a blue halo of light shining around his body and hands. The humanoid stepped away from the water, the glow around his body dimming until he looked like a slightly-taller-than-normal man with brown-tinted hair, honey-coloured eyes, a plain white t-shirt and jeans.

Ben pinched the tip of his friend's sleeve to confirm the clothing was dry even though Mesmo had just swum up from the bottom of the lake. He couldn't help wondering what it would have been like if he had had Mesmo's *water skill* instead of his own *translation skill*, but decided that, although it would have been cool to manipulate water, he much rather preferred being able to communicate with animals.

Man and boy stared at the calm lake.

"What do you think?" Ben asked, trying to spot Mesmo's spaceship hidden at the bottom.

Mesmo rested his hands on his hips. "This should do. Even if random hikers decided to go for a swim, the water's too deep for them to notice anything."

"It's October," Ben agreed. "It's not like anybody's going to swim here in the coming months. The water's way too cold."

Mesmo nodded in satisfaction. "Good."

"I still wish we'd found a spot closer to home."

"Why? Are you afraid of a little hike?"

Ben grimaced. "Very funny. Ha-ha. I never said I was afraid of a five hour hike."

Mesmo slapped his back. "So let's get going then. I don't want to be late for your mom's lasagna."

Ben shook his head as he slipped his parka through the strap of his backpack. "You sound way too human sometimes." He'd meant to sound sarcastic, but Mesmo broke into a smile as if Ben had just offered him a major compliment.

They set off away from the lake, Ben taking a longing glance back. He was going to miss travelling in Mesmo's spaceship.

"I still think it should be closer to home," he mumbled wistfully. He could think of a thousand reasons why one would need a sophisticated, advanced alien transport that could travel around the world or cross the Solar System at interstellar speeds.

"You know we can't leave it in the shed, Benjamin. We're lucky no-one came across it so far." Mesmo hopped across a rough patch of terrain and waited for Ben to catch up. "And to be truly successful in our mission," Mesmo continued, "We need to take things to a more *human* level. It would be unfair and unwise to influence human progress with Toreq technology. Humans need to reach a new level of consciousness on their own, without feeling the pressure of alien supremacy."

Ben's mind wandered as Mesmo spoke. Not because he didn't care or that he disagreed with his friend, but simply because his thirteen-year-old self just wanted to feel the thrill of flying in an alien spaceship again.

And anyway, Ben wondered if Mesmo was

giving him the whole story.

He had overheard Mesmo tell his mom that videos of the spaceship had emerged on social media, making it riskier to use the craft.

And so, that night, in the pounding rain, Ben had accompanied Mesmo in the spaceship in search of a better hiding spot for it. This last flight had only lasted about fifteen minutes.

Ben sighed.

Fifteen minutes to find this spot. And now a five hour long hike back...

The sun rose higher, cleaning the sky of clouds and illuminating a rugged landscape sprinkled with raindrops and dew. Water vapour escaped from patches of fir trees, new snow topped the tallest mountains surrounding them, and Ben spotted his hometown of Chilliwack, far down in the valley.

He breathed in the crisp air and decided this hike wasn't so bad. A peaceful day's walk was a welcome change to the hectic weeks he'd just experienced. He'd appeared in newspaper articles, done radio interviews, and made television appearances. He'd been shoved around from one studio to the other; talking to one reporter after another and answering questions about his skill.

He'd have to explain over and over that he

could communicate with animals. He'd have to repeat that, no, he wasn't making this up and, no, he wasn't crazy. But, despite his best efforts, his plea to help the natural world kept falling on deaf ears...

"Do you want to talk about it?" Mesmo said, startling Ben out of his thoughts. It was as if both had been mulling over the same things as they walked.

Ben knew Mesmo was referring to the last interview he'd had in Seattle on *Charlie's Chit-Chat Show.*

Another flop.

Ben had expected it. Even so, he couldn't help the embarrassment that came with every failed interview. He pushed down his feelings. "There's nothing to talk about," he said, walking past Mesmo, who had stopped to look at him.

"Benjamin," Mesmo said.

"What?"

"I think we should talk about it."

Ben slowed down. He stared at his muddy sneakers, then said, "It's okay, really. I knew nobody was going to take me seriously." He looked up at the tall alien. "But I have to keep trying." He put on a brave face for as long as he could manage, then turned and walked away so

Mesmo wouldn't see his eyes cloud up.

He knew Mesmo and his mom were worried about him. *Worried* was an understatement.

More like totally freaking out.

They hadn't scolded him once since he'd revealed his skill to the Provincial Times reporter, Jeremy Michaels. They supported him. His mom had driven him to all his interviews, cheered him on, spent long evenings going over what he could and couldn't say to the public. And Mesmo had taught him to control his skill. It was one thing to tell viewers he could talk to animals; it was another to have the alien skill seep out of his skin and glow a deep blue just like Mesmo's had a moment ago, by the lake.

Mesmo's patience and dedication, teaching Ben to use the skill without revealing its extraterrestrial source, had been liberating for Ben. He could now connect with animals without people noticing his blue aura. It still felt uncomfortable and unnatural, with the skill vibrating just beneath the skin, longing to flow free, but at least he could wander about without fearing it would burst out at the wrong moment.

"You did good, you know?" Mesmo said. "You were faced with an unexpected situation—the panicked horse. It could have thrown you off guard and unleashed your skill on live TV, yet you stayed calm and maintained control. Few Toreq your age could have managed that."

Ben blushed, feeling a warm rush inside. But he also knew Mesmo hadn't truly spoken his mind yet, so he stopped and asked, "Are you angry at me?"

Mesmo frowned. "Angry? Why would I be angry?"

Because I didn't tell you... Because now you're worried about me...

Lately, when they thought he'd gone to bed, Ben would overhear his mom and Mesmo talk in low, urgent whispers late into the night. They would debate how to best protect Ben and what impact the media would have on their lives. They worried that people would make a fool out of him—then, they worried when the press and public *did* make a spectacle of him.

Nobody truly believed a child could be an animal whisperer. Ben felt like he just fueled people's imaginations; that they longed for the animal whisperer to be true, but knew deep down that it was probably all part of a show.

Ben had overheard all this, sitting on the stairs, listening to his mom and Mesmo talking in the living room.

Yet, every morning, when Ben joined them for breakfast, they pretended everything was under control. They remained silent about what they were really feeling.

To protect me.

But now Ben wanted to know the truth. "Are you angry that I revealed my skill to the world without consulting you first?"

Mesmo leaned against a protruding rock. "I'm not angry, Benjamin," he said. "I'm disappointed. Do you want to know why I'm disappointed?"

Ben's shoulders slumped, but he nodded.

"I'm disappointed because you're facing this on your own, when you shouldn't be," Mesmo said. "I think you did the right thing. And I think I should be there with you, confirming your claims."

Ben's eyes widened. "Whoa! Wait a minute! Claiming I can understand animals is one thing, but announcing to the world that aliens have landed on Earth is another thing entirely! Humans have always had a connection with animals. My skill isn't too far-fetched. People think it's cute— harmless even. But aliens? That's kinda shocking. Revealing yourself could cause all kinds of serious problems. Things you couldn't even begin to imagine!"

Mesmo sighed. "Yes, I know. You sound like your mother. And you sound like Inspector Hao. But it's not fair for you to do this on your own. Your mother and the Inspector already know I will reveal myself as soon as the situation allows it."

"You can't do that, Mesmo! If people call me a freak, imagine what they'll call you? Have you already forgotten what happened last time? There's plenty of nasty people out there who would want to get their hands on you. Victor Hayward was just one of them."

Mesmo's voice came gently. "Then why did *you* do it, Benjamin?"

Ben started, taken aback. Mesmo had him cornered. He didn't want Mesmo to reveal himself to the world, but he had just done so himself.

Mesmo wanted the world to know that he was an alien and that his people, the Toreq, would one day threaten human existence. For the Toreq felt humans were an unworthy and dangerous species that should not be allowed to thrive in space or on other planets. Ben felt in his gut that revealing this information was a very, very bad idea. If people weren't ready to hear Ben's message of bringing balance to the natural world, how would they ever accept Mesmo's message of a possible alien invasion?

Not ever.

He could think of a thousand things that could go wrong. The mere thought of the danger his alien friend could put himself in, overwhelmed him.

He sighed because Mesmo had caught him in a dilemma, but answered, "Because I don't care if they call me a freak." He dropped down onto a boulder beside the alien. "They can call me anything they like. They can make fun of my skill, they can call me names and label me a phony, and they can laugh at my circus stunts." He looked up at Mesmo. "But this isn't about me. This goes beyond me. This is about our world and its survival. This is about making humans understand the needs of the other creatures that inhabit Earth." He nodded to himself. "So I'll make them listen, Mesmo. Even if it takes me the rest of my life."

Mesmo sat beside him. After a pause, he said, "Then you understand why I have to join you."

CHAPTER 3 *Making Plans*

"Are you watching the movie with us, Ben?" Laura asked.

Ben was putting a milk carton back in the fridge. "Which one is it?" he called, shutting the fridge door and grabbing the glass of milk he had just poured himself.

Laura set a steaming cup of tea on the coffee table and sat beside Mesmo. "We're watching *Titanic.*"

Ben almost choked on his milk. "Are you serious?"

"What's wrong with *Titanic*? It's very educational. Plus, Mesmo wants to understand the difference between movies that are based on real life and purely fictional ones."

"Mooom!" Ben groaned. "You're just making that up so you can watch your favourite actor. Couldn't you just watch *A Space Journey* or *Galaxy Hero* or something?"

"I watched those already, Benjamin," Mesmo said.

"Yes, and he thought they were real," Laura pointed out, eating a piece of popcorn. "Hence, the importance of determining what's real and what's fake on TV."

"Fine, whatever," Ben grumbled, placing his empty glass in the dishwasher and heading for the stairs. "I have a call with Kimi, so don't wait for me."

"Okay," Laura said. "Tell Kimi to ask her mom if she needs anything for next week," she shouted after him.

"Sure, Mom," Ben shouted back. As he reached the landing, he could already hear his computer pinging from Kimi's incoming messages. He rushed into his bedroom and clicked the 'answer' button before sliding into his desk chair.

A familiar face appeared on the screen.

"Hi, Kimi," Ben said.

"What took you so long?" his friend scolded, tying her long black hair into a ponytail.

"Mom wanted me to watch *Titanic* with them."

"Ugh," she said, sticking out her tongue. "That's so cheesy. It's like my mom and Thomas; they keep cooking together like they're on a date, with candles and everything. I swear, it cuts my appetite."

Ben laughed. He knew his friend didn't really mean what she said. She was thrilled that her mom had found a partner, and she was just being empathetic with him.

A boy's face appeared on the screen beside Kimi and blew mini-kisses at the camera.

Ben gagged. "Argh! Tyler, stop that!"

Kimi giggled.

Another boy appeared. "Hi, Ben," he said.

"Hi, Wes. How's it going?"

"Pretty good, actually. We're all done setting up your new website and nonprofit organization *great-gathering.org*. You're gonna be a *staaar*." He ended in a singsong voice.

Kimi leaned forward. "We can't wait to show you. It looks amazing!"

A fuzzy feeling filled Ben's heart. "Thanks, guys!"

"Hey, Wes," Tyler said, turning his attention away from the screen. "I think my mom's here.

We gotta go."

"Oh, okay... coming," Tyler's best friend said, fishing his backpack from the floor. "'Bye, guys." he waved.

"Yeah, 'bye guys!" Tyler chimed in from the door. "See you at Thanksgiving, Ben!"

Ben waved back at his old classmates even though the boys had gone.

A sudden silence fell over Kimi's room.

"Still bat-crazy, huh?" Ben said.

Kimi snorted. "Still bat-crazy. But they worked really hard. You'll love what they did. It's not going to be anything like *Charlie's Chit-Chat Show*. We're talking serious stuff now."

Ben's face slumped. "You saw that, huh?"

Kimi smacked her lips. "Of course, I did. I keep track of all your TV appearances and interviews. I'm sorry they didn't listen to your message, Ben."

Ben dropped his chin into his hands. "It's always the same. They treat me like I'm some kind of circus freak. They just want me to put on a good show."

"It's okay," she said soothingly. "We knew this was going to happen. People aren't ready to listen to the real message. But you just have to keep at it until they start realizing you're the real deal."

Ben yawned. "Not tonight, I won't."

"Just hang on a sec before you fall asleep on me," Kimi said. "I wanted to go over next week with you. So Thomas will fly his plane over to pick you up at 2 pm next Thursday, October 13th. He just needs to fill her up again, and then you'll all fly back to Canmore together."

Ben tried not to smile, remembering how nervous Mesmo had been in Thomas' small plane.

Kimi continued, "On Friday... um, my mom asked if you could lend a hand at her veterinary office. Did I tell you she opened her practice again?"

Ben straightened. "No, you didn't."

"Well, she did. She's super happy. Except, yesterday, they brought her a wounded cougar cub."

"No way!"

"Yeah, I know, right?" Kimi said. "Anyway, she was wondering if you could give her a hand with it. It's not exactly the usual type of patient that she gets."

"Sure thing!" Ben exclaimed, excitement surging at the upcoming long weekend in Canmore.

After Ben had become a bit of a media

sensation for his ability to communicate with animals, Kimi had offered to help him manage the flood of emails and letters he was getting. Most came from people who wanted him to teach them his skill. But Ben needed to get his real message across: 'The animals are sick and on the verge of mass extinction.'

It became imperative to be taken seriously because the Great Gathering that he and Mesmo were planning on holding on solstice day at the mouth of the Amazon River was fast approaching. The animals had assured Ben they would be there. But what about humans?

That's when Kimi came up with the brilliant idea of creating a nonprofit organization to help animals, along with a website and social media, where Ben would be able to deliver his message online until the right people paid attention to him.

"Okay, October 15th is Thanksgiving," Kimi continued. "So we'll have to help Mom and Thomas. But on the 16th, Wes and Tyler are coming over. We can film your message and work on the website."

"Maybe you could film me with the cougar," Ben suggested.

"Brilliant!" Kimi exclaimed. "I'm so excited, I've never celebrated Thanksgiving before."

"How come?"

"Not everyone sees Thanksgiving as a reason to celebrate, Ben. It's a reminder of a time when Westerners came to the Americas and caused centuries of suffering and death to the indigenous population."

"Ouch!" Ben breathed, at a loss for words as he realized he should have remembered this fact from history class.

"Don't look so sombre," Kimi grinned. "Mom said it was okay as long as we focus on celebrating the autumn harvest instead."

"Okay, cool. I like that," Ben said, feeling a bit overwhelmed, then remembering what he was supposed to ask. "Um, Mom wants to know if your mom needs us to bring anything."

"Thanks, I'll let you know. Now off to bed with you, sleepyhead. You look like you can't keep your eyes open."

He couldn't, but he didn't want to seem ungrateful. Thinking of the new website, he said, "Thanks, Kimi, for doing all of this for me."

"It's not for you, silly," she teased. "It's for the animals."

"Oh, right, of course." Ben grinned sheepishly.

"'Nighty-night, animal whisperer," she said.

"See you in four days."

"'Night, Kimi."

The screen went dark.

Ben gave a huge yawn. His comfy bed invited him over. He planned to lie down for just a minute, then brush his teeth and put on his pj's.

As he sank into the mattress, he briefly imagined his mom scolding him for not having done those things first. He yawned again and reached out to pet his dog.

"Night, Buddy," he mumbled to his black-and-white English Shepherd, who always sat by his bedside, waiting for an invitation to jump up and settle down beside him.

Except, Buddy wasn't there.

Ben opened his eyes and searched the room. "Buddy?" he called again, then listened for the familiar pitter-patter of the dog's feet on the floorboards.

The room was silent.

Ben sank into his pillow, thinking.

When had he last seen Buddy? Was the dog still outside?

He imagined the English Shepherd running after a rabbit through the cornfields.

Like last week. And the week before.

He groaned, in no mood to get up again.

Dragging himself off the bed, he put his hoodie back on and slipped his feet into his sneakers, pressing the back flaps under the heels of his feet as if they were slippers. The soles still had a thin layer of dry mud on them from the hike. He'd have to wash them tomorrow morning before his mom had a fit. He shuffled to the window, opened it, and stuck out his head.

"Buddy?" he called, scanning the darkness for the dog with his mind. The alien skill tingled in his hands.

CHAPTER 4 *Kidnapped*

Buddy's thoughts were usually lively and excited. Not so now. A whisper brushed through Ben's senses, and he craned his neck to look at the back of the house, where a night-light illuminated a patch of grass behind the kitchen.

Is that Buddy, lying there?

Ben spotted a dark form on the grass, but he couldn't tell if it was just a shadow, or maybe Mesmo had forgotten to put away the lawnmower. He figured it was the latter because if it had been Buddy, the dog would have barked by now.

Feeling worried, Ben pulled back and resolved to look for the dog by the cornfields. He hurried downstairs and thought about telling his mom, but both she and Mesmo were engrossed in their movie.

"So, these two people really existed on the Titanic?" Mesmo asked, referring to the man and woman actor dancing in a fancy hall on the screen.

"No," Laura giggled. "I mean, the actors exist, in real life, but here they are only pretending to be people who were on the Titanic."

"But how can they be on the Titanic, if it sank to the bottom of the ocean?"

Ben rolled his eyes. He did not want to be part of this conversation and wanted to find Buddy. Pushing at the kitchen door, Ben was surprised to find that the hinges no longer squeaked. *Mesmo must've fixed them.*

He was met by cold air. He wrapped his arms around his waist and watched his breath form before his face. He hadn't bothered to put on socks, so a chill seeped into his sneakers.

A weak whimper reached his ears, making his skin crawl.

"Buddy?" he gasped, rushing towards the black form he had spotted from his bedroom window earlier. It was Buddy, all right!

The dog lay sprawled on the ground, its breath shallow.

"Buddy, what's wrong?" Ben cried in fear. He

threw himself by the dog's side, scanning its body with his mind.

There was no pain. Instead, Buddy just seemed awfully tired.

The dog whined. Ben noticed a strange blob by Buddy's snout and leaned over to inspect it. It was a piece of half-eaten meat with a foul smell. Ben caught his breath. Had somebody deliberately tried to poison his dog?

Dread grasping his chest; he turned towards the house. "Mom! Come qui..." he shouted, but his voice died in his throat.

Two men loomed over him.

"Hey! Wha..." A strong hand clamped over his mouth. Another grasped his wrist. He struggled to break free, but a cloth pressed against his nose, quashing his yells and releasing a sweet, yet potent smell into his nostrils.

Ben's instincts flared. *Don't breathe in!*

Strong arms restrained him. Eyes blurred.

Don't brea...

He felt himself going limp. Drifting into darkness.

Somebody! Help!

* * *

The doomed ship tilted into the black ocean as its bow took on water.

"I wish I had been there," Mesmo said in a sombre voice. "I could have saved them, you know?"

Laura patted the back of his hand, wondering if it had been a good idea to show the alien this piece of sad history. "We'll see something more cheerful next time," she promised, leaning into him. A gust of air snuck into the house, making her shiver.

She turned and found the kitchen door open a crack. "Oh, Buddy," she scolded the absent dog. She got up and closed the door, happy to shut out the night.

Dull thuds cut the silence outside.

"Did you hear that?" Mesmo asked over the sound of screaming people on the TV screen. He lowered the volume.

"Car doors?" she asked, glancing his way.

Mesmo nodded, "Are you expecting anybody?"

She shook her head. The sound had come from nearby, but she had no close neighbours.

A motor roared to life.

"Somebody's here," Mesmo said, jumping up. He rushed to the front door and swung it open.

Tires screeched on the loose gravel.

"Mesmo? What is it?" Laura asked, more worried by Mesmo's alarmed attitude than by the car sounds.

"I don't know," Mesmo said, turning towards her. "Go check on Benjamin, will you?"

"Uh... O-okay..." Laura's chest squeezed. She leapt up the stairs and entered Ben's room. It was empty.

"Ben?" she called, crossing the room in a few strides and sticking her head out the open window. She was met with darkness and the stark rustling of wind through the cornfields... and a whimper.

Heart racing, she stretched her neck and spotted Buddy lying on the grass, near the kitchen. The dog lifted its head without getting up.

"Buddy!" she cried in alarm. "Mesmo! Something's wrong with Buddy!"

Mesmo came running around the house and knelt beside the dog.

"...and Ben's not in his room!" she said, her voice now thick with fear.

The alien reached for something beside the dog. He stood and turned towards her, holding up one of Ben's black sneakers.

CHAPTER 5 *Search*

There were few moments of clarity. Ben swung between consciousness and darkness—but mostly darkness. His senses picked up confusing signals, though never more than one at a time.

First, it was the smell of a dusty, slightly moist carpet—like the one in the trunk of his mom's car. It tickled his nostrils. Then, bright lights. Men's deep voices. A new smell. Wood, this time. Hard floor. Air coming through holes. A terrifying thought.

Oh God, I'm in a crate!

The blast of powerful engines. A roaring noise that shook him and lifted his stomach to his throat. He drifted into unconsciousness and dreamt he was at the back of Thomas' plane.

How was that possible? Had a week passed already? Was he on his way to Canmore?

"Thomas!" he yelled, only to find something stuck in his mouth. Ben blinked, and Thomas disappeared from his eyelids. Confusion. A terrible, sinking feeling in the pit of his stomach.

He struggled, but his hands were bound, and they banged against wooden boards. Primal fear threatened to engulf him.

This isn't Thomas' plane!

His feet were so cold! He curled into a ball and shivered for a long time.

Where am I?

Sudden, bright lights made him jolt. A man's face, speaking harshly. A warm blanket. A strong, sweet smell in his nostrils and a forced sleep...

The next time Ben came to, the sun heated his left cheek. His right cheek pressed against a cool car seat. Sunlight pierced into his eyes through a car window, making him moan. A man's arm reached out and covered his face with a blanket, then all he heard was the smooth sound of a car engine that went on for hours and hours.

It was strange, how settings changed after simply closing his eyes. Now he lay on something soft—a bed, maybe—and he just wanted to sleep, but two men's voices kept waking him. He opened his eyelids a crack and saw the blurry outline of a bulky man. He was arguing with another one over a smartphone or tablet. Their voices rose in anger.

Ben wished they would stop already; he was so tired. Trying to make sense of the conversation only worsened his throbbing headache, and he drifted into darkness again.

* * *

"Twenty hours!" Laura burst. "It's been twenty hours!" She paced back-and-forth, her face contorted in anguish.

"Laura," Mesmo took her by the shoulders. "I know this is hard, but we have to stay focused! It's the only way we'll find Ben."

Laura lifted her hands against his chest, fists balled. "Focused?" Her voice rose in panic. "How can I stay focused? Every minute we stand here, Ben is slipping further and further away from us!"

High Inspector James Hao hung up his phone and turned his attention to them. "We're doing all we can, Laura. We'll find Ben, I promise."

"I can't just stand here doing nothing. I... I've got to do something, I..." She broke off, her breath coming in short, rasping bursts. She shut her eyes.

Asthma attack!

The third one since Ben's kidnap. She hadn't had them in months and no longer had an inhaler.

Mesmo pulled her into his arms and held her tight.

She let herself go, concentrating on his soothing presence, and let her asthma attack run its course until she could control her breathing again.

He held her without saying anything.

When she was calm enough, she raised her head and looked at him.

"I'll find him," Mesmo said, eyes rock-hard with determination.

She believed him. She had to, for her sanity.

"Hello? Excuse me?" Someone shouted from the front door, making them all jump.

The outline of a lanky man with curly hair, and a bag strung over his shoulder filled the doorway.

"Jeremy!" Laura said.

The twenty-three-year-old reporter lifted the brown leather bag over his head and put it on the ground while presenting his ID to a police officer who stood guard by the door.

Feeling a ripple of hope, Laura whispered in Mesmo's ear, "It's okay, I called him. I can deal with him."

"Are you sure?" His eyes filled with worry.

She nodded.

He hesitated, then signalled towards Inspector Hao, and both men slipped away through the kitchen door.

Jeremy Michaels joined Laura in the living room, dumped his bag on the coffee table, then sat next to it. He fished out his camera, a notepad, and a pen. "Sorry it took me so long," he said, a little out of breath. "I was on assignment in Ottawa. Came back as soon as I could."

"Thank you, Jeremy," Laura said earnestly. She sagged into the couch opposite him and rested her forehead in the palm of her hands.

Buddy came over and rested his snout on her legs, looking forlorn.

"Don't worry, ma'am." Jeremy's voice softened. "We'll find your son. I can get an exclusive online article out within the hour. Half the continent will be looking for Ben by nightfall. Nobody would want to lose the *animal whisperer...*"

* * *

Mesmo and High Inspector James Hao from the Canadian Security Intelligence Service stepped away from the house with quick strides.

"Jeez'! You have to stop doing things without consulting me!" Hao snapped, combing his military-cut black-and-grey hair with his hand. "You *are* aware that that reporter has been hounding me about *The Cosmic Fall* for weeks, aren't you? Next thing he'll be hounding you, too…"

Mesmo placed his hands on his hips. "I understand, Inspector. Believe me, I do. But we can't afford to be picky right now. Jeremy Michaels is the one who 'revealed' the *animal whisperer* to the world. He's in a perfect position to draw a crowd to his article. We'll need all the eyes we can get to find Ben."

"You think I don't know that?" Hao argued. "I just wish you'd told me first. It was complicated enough when Ben blurted out his story to the media. I warned you that pulling off something like that could put you and Ben in danger." He breathed out heavily. "Turns out I was right." He bit his lip, shaking his head, then glanced at the police officers combing the backyard. He sighed and massaged the bridge of his nose with his fingers. "I apologize." His voice softened. "This is no time to be pointing fingers. But I just wish you and Ben listened to me once in a while. I *do* actually know what I'm talking about when it comes to personal and national security."

"You're right," Mesmo said. "I promise to pay more attention. Tell me how I can help."

Hao pursed his lips for a moment. "That's the problem," he admitted. "We have no leads yet. The kidnappers left no fingerprints. We have tire tracks, but without road cameras in the area, it will take some time to identify the car. We're sifting through film data from neighbouring towns, narrowing down the time of Ben's disappearance. We'll check every vehicle that passed through the area.

"I've also set up a team on the thousands of emails Ben got after his TV appearances. You never know whom he could have upset. Something's bound to come up." He paused to think, then added. "One thing's for sure. Ben wasn't taken by any foreign power. I have confirmation of the highest level."

Mesmo grimaced. "...because foreign countries would tell you that, willingly?"

"We're following all leads, Mesmo. That includes asking other governments what their position is. If they lied, it would tarnish their image."

Mesmo stared at the cornfields, deep in

thought.

"What?" Hao said. "Is there something else I should know?"

Mesmo rubbed his chin, then pointed in the direction of the fields. "On the night of *The Cosmic Fall*," he began, "Two spaceships crashed into these fields. The third one landed. I hid the third spaceship in the mountains yesterday. But what about the other two?" He turned to face Hao. "I trust your government didn't send them to the scrap yard?"

Hao snorted at the jab. "You know humans better than that, Mesmo. Who do you take us for? Of course, they didn't end up in the scrap yard. We've managed to assemble a pretty decent replica from the salvaged parts. Pasted together with super glue and tape..."

"Really?" Mesmo said with interest, not catching on to Hao's joke. "And, does it fly?"

"Of course not! We have no idea where the start button is. Unless you finally agreed to show us. Or you give us a hint, at least."

"Actually, I can tell you more than that. You see, the pilot *is* the start button, so to speak."

Hao raised an eyebrow. "Meaning...?"

Mesmo smiled sadly. "Sorry, Inspector. Only Toreq men and women can fly Toreq spaceships.

It's something that dates back to the *Great War of the Kins*. The Toreq couldn't afford to have the A'hmun—your human ancestors—manipulate our space fleet." He paused, then added, "No offence."

"None taken, I'm sure," Hao growled. "And, uh, what does this spaceship have to do with Ben, exactly?"

Mesmo stared across the cornfields again. "Nothing at all," he said. "Or maybe everything."

CHAPTER 6 *Isolated*

Ben knew he should wake up, but he didn't want to.

There was something comfortable and reassuring about lingering in the space between sleeping and waking, but he could also feel it, at the edge of his mind. Just beyond his eyelids: a sharp migraine awaited him. And a terrible, terrible awareness.

His stomach flipped.

Not just yet...

He couldn't handle it just yet. He felt safer in his half-sleep, lulled by gentle, repetitive waves of warm air that caressed his cheeks. Light linen covered his body, and his head rested on a soft cushion.

He opened his eyelids a fraction and stared at the brown ceiling fan, its blades turning in a constant motion that almost put him to sleep again.

I wish I had a ceiling fan at home...

The thought jolted him.

I'm not at home!

The realization hit him like a hammer. He sat up straight, heart pounding.

The room swam before his eyes, followed by the promised headache that made him groan. He shut his eyes, focusing on his breathing, then peeked through his eyelids once the thudding lessened.

He took in his surroundings.

A large room. Beige walls. A gold-coloured bed cover, linen sheets with gold-coloured cushions on a king bed, an upholstered bench at its foot. To his right, an arched mirror next to a door, which was closed. To his left, another door leading to a marble-floored bathroom. Before him, heavy drapes of a luxurious darker-gold colour were pulled to the side of two wide windows. The windows were covered by semi-transparent curtains that blew gently from a breeze that came either from the ceiling fan or from outside. Next to the windows stood a dark-wood closet that matched the bed and bench and presented intricate designs—a bit like lace.

Ben pushed the bedsheet off his body and found himself fully-dressed. There was a tear in his hoodie, his jeans were stained with dirt, and there were scratches on his wrists. Other than that, he seemed whole and functional. Swinging his legs over the bed's edge, he stepped onto the cool marble floor and tested his muscles. He felt a bit woozy, but it was manageable, so he stepped to the windows and pushed the curtains aside.

Given how rich and how lush the room was, the view outside turned out to be disappointing. Ben stared at a high, outer wall followed by a dusky sky. The sand-coloured wall ran the full length of the view, from left to right, and possibly continued around the building or house.

Ben tested the windows. They were locked.

Fending off a surge of panic, he stepped back, closed his eyes and took quick gulps of air. Nothing looked familiar. Nothing made sense.

Where am I?

He opened his eyes and found a set of white cotton clothes folded on the upholstered bench. Just below the bench, leather sandals with wavy lines and dots had been placed side by side. And next to them, a single black sneaker. *His* sneaker!

He picked it up, eager to have found something familiar. He bent down and searched under the bed for the other sneaker, but it wasn't there.

The heat in the room made his head sway and pound again. He was sweating, and he wished someone would lower the heating.

Standing with his one sneaker in hand, Ben glanced around the room and spotted a small table under the mirror. There was a jug of water with lemon slices in it, and a glass beside it. Ice cubes still floated on the surface of the water, meaning it had been left there not too long ago.

Ben slipped on the one sneaker and hobbled across the room. He grabbed the jug, not even bothering with the glass, and lifted it to his cracked lips. Then he froze. A fearsome image of an inert Buddy flashed before his eyes.

What if it's not just water?

He stood still for a couple of seconds, then put the jug down slowly. Swallowing through a desert-dry throat, he turned his attention to the door.

Locked, for sure.

He reached for the handle with a trembling hand and turned it.

The door swung inward, startling him.

His heart raced again. Could it be that

simple? Maybe it was all a mistake. Maybe he was supposed to be here but just couldn't remember why. He wasn't sure he wanted to stay and find out, though.

He peeked out the bedroom door and glanced up and down a long, empty corridor. The walls were the same beige colour as his room. On his left, the corridor was cut by wide archways with hazy sunlight streaming through them.

A way out?

Maybe. Maybe not.

And the heat? Well, there clearly wasn't an issue with the heating system because the heat didn't come from *inside* the building. It came from *outside.*

He checked the corridor again, then, not hearing anything, prepared to hop awkwardly towards the archways.

Don't be stupid.

The one sneaker felt like a lifeline, but it was slowing him down. He tossed it back into the room, then dashed down the corridor, his bare feet slapping on the marble floor.

The archways led into a large patio surrounded by equally arched corridors and doors at regular intervals. Tall palm trees reached for the sky, and in the centre, a small, mouthwatering fountain bubbled cheerfully. Ben had trouble ignoring it, but his gut feeling told him to move on.

As he crossed the patio, glancing nervously around him, he took in his strange surroundings. What place had scorching weather like this in the middle of the fall? California? *Mexico?* That would explain the palm trees and arched patio.

Ben wiped the sweat from his brow, afraid to linger on the thought that getting home might not be that simple. How the heck had he gotten this far without anyone noticing? Who had the power to do something like this?

Voices echoed down the corridor behind him.

Ben jerked, panic taking over. He sprinted to the other side of the patio, which ended in the same adobe wall he had seen from his bedroom window. Only, this one had a wooden door in it. And it was ajar!

A way out!

He'd find a village, a town—people. Anyone! He'd get help, find out where he was. This nightmare would be over.

His hopes lifting, Ben pressed against the door with his shoulder since it was only open a crack, and pushed.

It wouldn't budge.

The voices neared.

Ben pushed harder. Something was holding the door back, like accumulated earth from years of neglect. He could hear the dirt crunching and shifting under his weight.

The approaching men were a breath away from discovering him.

Frantic, Ben slammed into the door with all his might. It gave way, swinging open. He lost his footing and tumbled through, landing on the other side.

Rolling back in a haste, he reached out and kicked the door closed with his foot, in the nick of time.

The men entered the patio, laughing and chatting, ignorant of his presence behind the wall. Ben sank on his back, relieved to have something solid separating him from his mysterious captors.

Heat beat down on him. He sat up, trying to ignore the throbbing in his head, then shielded his eyes with his arm.

And stared. Dumbstruck.

His mind numbed in disbelief. His California theory crashed down on him.

Mounds of sand stretched before him, from left to right, far into the horizon.

He stared again, looking for an explanation, but his eyes were unable to convey to his brain what he was seeing.

This isn't right. This can't *be right!*

Shocked, Ben stepped onto scorching sand and climbed up a dune that felt as tall as a mountain. His bare feet sank deep, the sand burning the soles of his feet, making his progress slow and hard, but dread spurred him on until he was high enough to take in his surroundings.

He straightened and gawked. Dunes to the east, dunes to the west. More to the south and north. Dunes everywhere. Like an ocean, but one made of sand instead of water. And in the middle of it all, to his right, a calm oasis of adobe buildings, sprinkled with green palm trees between them.

A hazy sky, which was the same colour as the desert, partially blocked out the sun. A sweltering wind lifted sand across the dunes, prickling Ben's cheeks.

And there was only silence. No sounds of voices, cars, or planes flying overhead. Only an endless emptiness devoid of noise and bustling life.

Forget Canada, forget California and Mexico. No place that he knew of on the

American continents looked like this.

Ben forgot to breathe. He had escaped one prison only to land straight in a new one. He wasn't going home. He was stuck in the middle of the desert—alone.

CHAPTER 7 *An Imposed Mission*

A falcon screeched high in the veiled sky, but Ben was too distraught to connect to his skill. His eyes stung from the sand, and his brain was numb from shock. The more he searched for a sign, something, anything familiar, the more he sank into despair. Not even Mesmo's alien knowledge would find him in this remote place.

When his feet could no longer stand the burning sand, he half-hopped, half-slid back down the dune and sank into a sliver of shadow offered by the adobe wall, hunching in on himself.

No wonder no one was watching him. No wonder the bedroom door wasn't locked. It wasn't necessary: the desert was his prison.

He shivered in spite of the heat, unable to

accept his new reality.

I was kidnapped. Kidnapped!

It wouldn't sink in. How had he let this happen? Why hadn't he reacted?

I should have shouted. Kicked. Something!

The two looming men surged in his mind.

No!

His stomach constricted. If he had shouted, he'd have put Mom and Mesmo in danger.

Tears threatened to pour out of his eyes.

Who did this? Why?

A new wave of panic surged through his mind. What if this had to do with Mesmo? What if they knew about the alien?

He shut his eyes.

Think!

No. Not Mesmo.

No one knew about Mesmo except himself, his mom, and Inspector Hao. Hao had assured his superiors that the alien had fled Earth in his spaceship after destroying the Dugout. No one knew that Mesmo had returned.

That left the seven Wise Ones. Could this have something to do with them? Some of them had rejected Mesmo because he had returned to Earth. They said he had turned his back on his people. Maybe this was some kind of retribution, a way to make Mesmo do whatever they wanted.

Ben wouldn't allow it. He wouldn't! He'd fight!

The pain in his feet became hard to ignore. He looked down and caught his breath. The soles of his feet had become a blistering red.

Heat smothered him. Sweat pearled on his forehead, and his hoodie felt unbearable. He peeled it off and covered his head with it, but this did little to cool him off.

Despair and fear seeped into his mind, but he knew he had no choice: he had to go back to his golden jail before he roasted in the desert. He stood and opened the door in the adobe wall, then entered the patio again, still shaking from shock.

He limped across the patio, dragging his hoodie along, and reached the glorious shade of the archways, then headed back into the main corridor.

A man with a brown beard, a white cloth headdress, and a white, long-sleeved tunic that dropped to his ankles, stood before the bedroom door. He rushed toward Ben, taking him by the arm and helping him hobble to his bed. He bent over to examine the boy's feet. The man shook his head, eyebrows drawing together as he scolded Ben in a foreign language.

Ben's mind did a double flip.

Arabic! This guy's speaking Arabic!

Not that he understood what the man was saying, but now the architecture, the furniture, the man's robes and—of course—the desert, suddenly made sense.

I'm in... Northern Africa? The Sahara Desert?

Ben swallowed a sob. The idea that he might be on a different continent altogether, in the middle of the biggest desert on Earth, made his muscles go limp. He almost passed out, but the man tapped his cheek, held him up into a half-sitting position, and gave him a glass of the lemon water.

Ben grabbed the glass feverishly with both hands and gulped down the cool fluid that trickled to his every limb.

Still talking, the man rushed out of the room, leaving the door wide open behind him—a gesture which now infuriated Ben. The man then returned with a tray and helped Ben sit up by adding a pile of cushions behind his back, then placing the tray over Ben's legs. Strong smells rose from a richly filled plate of food, which the man gestured towards. Ben's throat was too closed up with emotion to be able to eat, but he was also too weak to argue, so he tore a piece of flatbread and stuck it in his mouth. It tasted like parchment in his still dry mouth. He tried to swallow but couldn't. His feelings welled up and threatened to burst.

The man let him be. He disappeared again and quickly returned, holding a bowl. He sat on the edge of the bed and applied a creamy substance from the bowl on to Ben's feet. A cold and soothing feeling spread from his soles to his ankles.

Overcome by the shocks of the day, drowsiness spread to Ben's heavy eyelids, which closed without him even realizing it.

* * *

Someone shook Ben by the shoulder, startling him awake.

The bearded man with the cloth headdress gestured for him to get up.

Worry lines on the man's brow made Ben sit in a hurry, a new flood of fear washing over him. "What's going on?" he asked, knowing full well he would not understand the answer. He glanced around, despair grasping him as his new reality hit him again. He wondered whether he had slept another day away, but the food tray still sat on the small table under the mirror.

The man gushed in Arabic, waving his hands about. When he saw Ben didn't react, he frowned in concentration, wrung his hands together and said a single word, "Master."

Ben's skin crawled.

The man pointed to the door and repeated, "Master."

Ben swallowed. Was he on his way to meet his captor?

The man talked non-stop and unfolded the cotton clothes on the upholstered bench, waving them in Ben's face, and Ben realized it was a similar tunic fit for him.

Ben shook his head, adamantly. If he was going to meet the man who had forcefully brought him here, he was going to tell him a piece of his mind and demand to be taken home at once. There was no need to change into some other clothing.

He ignored how absurd his thoughts sounded, but needed to cling on to this shred of hope.

Because I'm going home.

The bearded man—who Ben now considered to be his appointed guard-slash-chaperone didn't seem happy that Ben wouldn't change, but it became clear he didn't have time to argue.

Ben had to give in to one thing, though. He reluctantly put on the sandals that had been left for him and was surprised to find they fit like a glove. The thought that someone had had these made especially for him made his stomach knot because it was another indication that his kidnapping had been planned for some time. He clenched his teeth and forced himself to accept the sandals. It wouldn't do to come across a chance of escape and find himself barefoot in the burning sand again.

The chaperone waved Ben over to the door, repeating, *"Yallah! Yallah!"* Ben figured it meant something like *hurry up!* They rushed down the corridor, passed the arched patio, then arrived in a wide lobby. Sofas with dark red cushions were placed in the center on a lush maroon carpet. Arabian lights and painted calligraphy ornamented the high ceiling.

Ben took in everything at a glance, frantically searching for something that could help him escape. Could he make a run for it? *But, run where?* Or what if he could hide instead? *And then what?*

He fought to put one foot before the other,

catching hurried glimpses of his surroundings through waves of panic. It took all of his willpower not to dash off, away from the chaperone, away from this *master* who had the power to transport him half-way across the world, undetected. But nothing helpful came to mind.

To his right: big, glass doors led to a terrace with interlacing arches and columns, then a wide staircase was followed by a flat stretch of sand, and, at the end of it stood an oasis of palm trees that looked like an island in the middle of the desert.

To his left: identical glass doors leading to the outside. The whole wall was made up of windows covered in laced shutters to soothe the glaring sunlight. In the distance, he glimpsed golden gates.

The main entrance!

Ben almost broke into a compulsive run at the sight, but just then, two guards marched before the glass doors.

Ben almost tripped over himself. If only he could think straight, but his brain was a whirlpool of distress, and he realized he risked making rash decisions that could get him in even more trouble.

"Yallah!!" the chaperone said again, before

stopping to open a wide set of doors that led to a huge dining room. A long, perfectly polished dining-table lay beneath Arabian-styled lamps and was surrounded by arched columns. On the left, windows led to the crushing scenery of endless dunes.

The light from outside was so bright, Ben did not immediately realize that a bulky man was sitting on a leather sofa to his right. A servant poured the man tea from an Arabian teapot that could have come straight out of Aladdin's cave. When he finished, the servant straightened, looked at Ben, and waved him over.

Ben's chaperone bowed and left the room.

The servant stretched out his hand, indicating that Ben should sit on a similar sofa opposite the bulky man; and then filled a second teacup that released a distinct aroma Ben couldn't quite identify.

Ben swallowed through his dry throat, hoping they couldn't hear his heart beating like a drum. He sat opposite the bulky man, trembling, and stared at his captor.

The bearded man must have been in his sixties. He wore a dark blue tunic and a red-and-

---

[1] Yallah = Arabic meaning, "Let's go, hurry up."

white checkered headdress. A black double-corded ringlet held the headdress in place. The half-scowl on the bulky man's face told Ben he was not looking forward to this conversation, and indeed, he turned to the servant and spoke to him without even acknowledging the teen.

"Benjamin Archer," the servant said, startling Ben. "You are the honoured guest of Sheikh Azhar bin-Rahman. He welcomes you to his humble home."

Ben's mind did a double-flip.

Guest? Humble?

The Sheikh said something more, to which the servant straightened and translated, "Your reputation precedes you. My honourable master says he is fortunate to have such a talented guest in his house."

Ben sank into the couch, dumbfounded. A Sheikh? He'd been kidnapped by *a Sheikh*?

His mind whirled.

Say something!

What was his plan of action?

Fight! Don't give in!

"You won't get away with this. If this is about Mesmo, you won't get anything out of me. Not if my life depends on it!" he blurted out.

The servant blinked.

The Sheikh wanted a translation.

Ben sat back and crossed his arms.

There! Let it be clear!

The servant-slash-interpreter made a little coughing sound and smiled politely. "I beg your pardon. My English is not so good. I do not know what is a mesmo. We do not have mesmos here."

Ben flushed. Unable to hold in his frustration, he snapped, "You had me kidnapped! I want to be taken home at once!" His voice wavered. "Or... or else..." His voice died in his throat.

Or else... what?

So much for a lasting impression. He'd meant to sound threatening, but these men and what they were capable of intimidated him more than he cared to admit.

The interpreter's face fell. He bent forward, swiftly dumping a couple of sugar cubes in Ben's tea. "I would not talk like that to the Sheikh," he warned in a low voice. "Or he will have you flogged."

Spiders crawled up and down Ben's spine. He glanced at the sullen Sheikh, whose glazed eyes were aimed at a spot above Ben's head.

Ben gulped. He believed the interpreter, which only served to add an extra layer of dismay to his already precarious situation.

The interpreter straightened and smiled. "The honourable Sheikh has important business to attend to outside the estate. We must therefore speed up this meeting. In any case, I take it you are as eager as he is to discuss the reason for your privileged encounter. So forgive me for getting straight to the point.

"Sheikh Azhar bin-Rahman has an only son, the beloved Zayed bin-Rahman. For his son's birthday, the Sheikh procured a priceless gift: an Arabian steed of the highest and most noble kind, called Sadalbari.

"The horse, however, is a wild soul and has not yet accepted its rider." He paused and gave Ben a meaningful look. "You will do the Sheikh a great honour by telling Sadalbari to allow Zayed to mount him."

Ben stared, stunned. The wheels in his brain had trouble turning. Had he heard correctly? "You... you brought me all the way out here to help a boy ride his new horse?"

The servant showed a row of white teeth. "That is correct. Once Sadalbari is mounted, the Sheikh will see you home on a first-class flight, and you will be paid a handsome sum for your services."

Ben's thoughts fell into a complete jumble. Out of every reason he had imagined for his kidnapping, this was by far the most bizarre one he could have come up with.

He gaped at the Sheikh and his interpreter.

The Sheikh humphed and stood heavily as if the conversation had bored him. The interpreter stepped aside nimbly. As if on cue, the dining-room doors opened, and two guards took place on each side.

It took a few seconds for Ben's brain to catch up. "No," he breathed, jumping from his chair, the interpreter's words barely sinking in. "Wait a minute I... I don't have time to teach a boy to ride his horse. I have to be in Canmore by the 15th! And, besides, I've never even ridden a horse myself..."

The Sheikh was already by the door.

The interpreter tailed the Sheikh, then turned to Ben. "The Sheikh will not be satisfied until his beloved son's wish is fulfilled. He trusts you will be as skillful as the media claim you to be. However, in his wisdom, the Sheikh understands the difficulty of your task. Therefore, you are welcome to stay for as long as it takes."

The interpreter's words tumbled over Ben like a bucket of ice.

For as long as it takes...

He could hardly find his voice. "W-Wait! You... you can't keep me here against my will! That's illegal! You... you can't do this!"

The Sheikh had already disappeared down the corridor. The interpreter glanced at Ben, both guards standing on either side of him. He was no longer smiling. "Zayed bin-Rahman has heard of your great power. He looks forward to seeing your talents upon his return from his ocean retreat next week. Do not deceive him." He turned on his heels and left.

Ben stood aghast. "Next week..." he gasped. *"Next week?"* His voice rose with every word. "Hey! You can't keep me here until next week! You... you can't!"

He threw himself forward, but one of the guards shoved him in the chest, making him stagger back. The doors shut on him with a bang.

"HEY!" he yelled, throwing himself at the door.

The bolt locked.

"HEY! Let me out! HEY!"

CHAPTER 8 *Golden Jail*

"Inspector, please tell us you have some good news," Laura said, facing her computer in the living room.

Inspector Hao's face was grave on the screen.

Laura turned to find Mesmo arriving through the kitchen door. They exchanged a glance. He gave a small shake of his head, indicating it had been another unsuccessful day of searching.

He joined her on the couch, and they both watched as someone handed Hao some paperwork on the screen.

Hao sighed. "Listen, we found a trace, but I don't want to get your hopes up."

Laura's heart beat faster. "What? What did

you find?"

Hao pursed his lips, maybe trying to judge whether she was ready to hear the news. Then, he said, "I don't think Ben is in Canada."

Laura caught her breath. The blood drained from her face as she tried to grasp the meaning of what Hao had just said.

"What do you mean?" she managed.

Hao looked over some papers. "We found the car that took off on the night of Ben's disappearance. The mud and tracks from the tires match those we found outside your house. A Lucas Brook and David Carter rented the car. There's no sign of them in any national or international systems. Fake names and fake IDs, by all accounts." He paused to glance at them.

Laura knew there was more. "Go on!" she urged, squeezing Mesmo's hand so hard it hurt.

"Well, we found the car..." Hao said. "...at the international airport."

Laura gasped.

Hao seemed reluctant to continue. He cleared his throat and said, "I won't sugarcoat things, Laura. The car was abandoned on the tarmac next to a private jet headed for the Canary Islands. The same men hired the plane."

"The Canary Islands? But, isn't that on the

other side of the Atlantic Ocean?" Mesmo burst.

Hao nodded. "Yes. The Canary Islands are a string of islands located off the coast of Morocco, in Northern Africa, but they actually belong to Spain."

Laura shut her eyes and swallowed. Mesmo's voice sounded far away.

"Wait a minute," Mesmo said. "How do you even know Ben was in that car?"

Laura peeked at the screen and saw Hao glance her way. "We found strands of Ben's hair in the trunk of the car."

Laura felt faint. Her head dropped against Mesmo's shoulder.

"...and, what else?" Mesmo insisted, his voice heavy.

"That's it, I'm afraid," Hao said. "The jet refuelled on the Canary Islands and took off again. The local airport manifest states the jet was headed for Athens, Greece, but there's no trace of it landing there."

"What is that supposed to mean?" Mesmo sounded angry. "Don't human airplanes have to land at some point?"

Hao's voice sounded hollow. "It means— Mesmo—that I don't think they were headed for Greece." He paused, "Which, in short, means Ben could be anywhere."

* * *

Ben ran around the dining-room like a trapped hare. Back-and-forth, back-and-forth. Searching for a way out. Testing the door. Testing every single window.

Locked. All of them.

He considered swinging a chair through a window, but the ebony chair was too heavy. And anyway, beyond the window, stretched miles of desert.

He sank to his knees, fighting not to cry.

I will not cry!

He bit into his balled fist.

Think!

A vivid image of Mesmo searching for him everywhere... His mom, dying with worry... These thoughts sprang into his mind without warning—so raw his heart could barely take it.

Waves of panic.

He fought to calm down, then forced himself to think again—but that only led him to a conclusion that made his stomach roil.

Because this wasn't about Mesmo. This wasn't about the Toreq, the A'hmun, *The Cosmic*

Fall or the Wise Ones. This wasn't about animals dying or anything else related to his and Mesmo's mission.

Far from it.

This was something else entirely. There would be no ransom, no demands, no negotiating. And that meant there would be no contact with home.

Tears finally spilled down his cheeks.

Ben was on his own.

* * *

"You have to get some sleep, Laura," Mesmo said gently.

He placed a glass of water on the coffee table and knelt beside her as she lay on the couch, her eyes lost in the distance, the knuckles of her fingers white from grasping the cushion too hard.

"Laura," he repeated, stroking a mesh of ash-blonde hair from her cheek. "You haven't slept in days. Even I know humans need a certain amount of rest to function properly."

"...can't," she mumbled, still staring into space.

He stroked her cheek, and their eyes finally connected.

"I can't, Mesmo," she breathed. "He's not sleeping, either. I just know it! Ben needs me! What if he reaches out..." Her eyes fell on her phone on the coffee table.

"Shh!" Mesmo said, sinking into a sitting position on the carpet. "I'm not going anywhere. If he calls, I'll be right here."

They held each other's gaze. He could tell she was reluctant to close her tense eyes, so he watched over her until she finally gave in to exhaustion. And even then, he sat beside her and waited until her breathing deepened.

Then, he stood quietly and pulled a blanket over her. He made sure her new asthma pump was next to the glass of water, then picked up both smartphones and headed outside through the kitchen door.

Buddy met him half-way across the lawn, wagging its tail and giving a small whine. Mesmo gave the dog a good rub on the head, then checked that he was out of earshot. He flipped open his phone and glanced at his missed calls.

They all came from the same number.

He pressed the call button and listened to the ringing tone on the other end.

"*Amigo²*, I was getting worried," a familiar

voice whispered.

"Amaru," Mesmo answered. "Forgive me. Things have been a little hectic." He stopped there because judging from the half-dozen missed calls, Mesmo already knew Amaru had news for him. "Did you find Einar?" he asked.

"Honestly, Mesmo, when you called and told me you suspected Einar of kidnapping Ben, I thought you'd gone *loco*!" Amaru's voice was as heavy as lead. "But as it turns out, things are about to get a lot more hectic."

"What do you mean?"

Amaru caught his breath on the other end. "Mesmo," he said. "Su Tai is dead!"

Mesmo froze.

"Did you hear me?" Amaru's voice wavered.

"What do you mean: Su Tai is dead?" Mesmo hissed. Cold sweat formed on his back. A Wise One, *dead*?

Amaru breathed hard into the phone as if he didn't want anyone to overhear him. "Listen carefully. The official cause of death states Su Tai died of a heart attack. But his daughter got ahold

---

[2] *Amigo* = Spanish for 'friend'.

[3] *Loco!* = Spanish meaning 'crazy, mad.'

of me. She suspects there was foul play."

Mesmo's mouth went dry. "Foul play?"

"She wouldn't elaborate, but she swears her father did not pass away from natural causes. She said she's gone into hiding and told me to do the same. At first, I wasn't sure, Mesmo. We both know Su Tai's health wasn't good. But then..." his voice faltered.

"What, Amaru?"

"Mesmo," the Bolivian said. "I... I can't get ahold of Akeya!"

Mesmo's ears rang, and he had to shut his eyes.

"Mesmo?" Amaru's voice came from far away. "Did you hear me? Akeya isn't picking up. It's not like her!"

Mesmo lifted his hand to his face, a surge of dread mounting to his neck.

"What's going on, Mesmo?" Amaru said.

* * *

Someone unlocked the dining-room door and placed a plate on the table. Rich smells of a finely cooked meal reached Ben's nostrils.

Countless hours had passed. Ben had ended up sitting on a chair at the dining table with his forehead pressing down against his hands, staring down at his feet. He didn't look up and pretended to sleep. He didn't want to give whoever was there the satisfaction of seeing his puffy, red eyes.

The person left.

Ben risked a glance over his shoulder and found the doors wide open.

But then, why wouldn't they be?

He stared at the plate, then pushed it away. Feeling detached and unable to make sense of anything, Ben plodded back to his appointed bedroom. He walked mechanically to his bed and curled up into a ball, feeling drained and helpless. Before he could help it, a feverish sleep took ahold of him and trapped him in shifting nightmares.

He woke up at the crack of dawn, feeling more confused and empty than ever. Needing to get away from his restless slumber, he slipped on the sandals and stepped into the corridor, then walked around, searching for a miracle solution to his plight.

The chit-chatting voices of women and the sounds of metal utensils reached his ears.

He found the source of the sounds and entered a bustling kitchen, full of unknown smells and ingredients. An older woman in a colourful dark-green dress with gold embroidery snapped a kitchen towel at him, scolding him in Arabic as she ushered him out again.

He was barely out the door and on to a patio when he realized she was following him. She made him sit on a small, adobe bench cut out in the wall, then disappeared into the kitchen.

Ben was going to slip away when a voice reverberated across the dunes—sudden and strong.

Goosebumps rose on Ben's arms. He'd never heard a voice like that before. He stood and stepped to the end of the patio. On the far end of the property, he spotted a small turret with a circular terrace at the top. The voice came from loudspeakers. The sounds in the kitchen stopped, and even the birds fell silent.

Ben listened in fascination, then realized this was something they did in Islamic countries.

A call to prayer...

Ben stood still until the voice fell silent. By now, the property was bathed in bright, morning light. Then the woman was there again, waving him back to the bench. She had placed a narrow carpet on it, topped with comfortable dark-red cushions. She then placed a tray laden with food in front of him: scrambled eggs, a type of pancake, something that looked like liquid yogurt and lamb meat with dates.

The aromas made Ben's head sway, and he realized he hadn't eaten in what felt like days. The woman stepped back, crossed her arms, and waited.

Heat rose to Ben's cheeks under her stern glare. Feeling like a kid who had just been reprimanded, Ben lifted a small cup containing a dark liquid and gulped it down. It turned out to be robust, spicy coffee that made his eyes water and jolted him awake.

There was no cutlery on the silver tray. He glanced at the woman, who indicated he should eat with his right hand. Under her watchful eye, Ben tasted everything and, to his surprise, finished the plate clean. He leaned back with a full belly.

The woman hadn't moved an inch.

"Uh... Thank you. That was delicious," Ben offered meekly.

She gave a small, satisfied nod, grabbed the tray and was gone.

Ben's spirit lifted considerably. He'd never had coffee before, and the strong brew tingled in his brain, making his thoughts sharp and focused. He wouldn't let himself go like that again, he vowed. He needed to be strong and alert if he was going to get out of here.

Mesmo's voice filled his head. "Concentrate, Benjamin! You'll know what to do."

Ben needed to be more like Mesmo: think in a cool and calm manner, study the situation from an analytical point-of-view. A chance of escape could very well be around the corner, and he needed to be ready when it came.

With that in mind, Ben climbed up and down half-hidden stairways, intent on studying his surroundings. The property was comprised of several small, rectangular homes, with the largest one in the middle. Together, these structures formed a rough half-moon. The oasis closed off the circle.

Everything was made of sand-coloured adobe, with arched windows, high ceilings, protruding wooden beams and flat roofs. Houses were separated by corridors or short, narrow streets that ended in stairways. The whole thing was a bit confusing at first until Ben learned to rely on the oasis to determine in which direction he was going. He had almost finished scouting the left side of the property when a familiar rushing sound coursed through his ears. His hands began to tingle.

The sound of neighing came from the end of a passage between two houses.

Ben turned the corner and found himself at the top of a set of stairs leading to a round, open clearing surrounded by a fence and flanked by a row of benches set in the shadow of a circular roof. A beautiful, elegant horse trotted around the clearing, a trainer clicking his tongue as he led the purebred from the center. Behind the clearing stood a large building that looked like a stable.

Ben's heart pumped harder.

That's it!

Maybe that horse—what was its name? *Sadalbari*—was in there. Maybe he could have a word with it, so he could be on his way.

CHAPTER 9 *Separation*

Mesmo descended the stairs and found Laura staring up at him, her eyes hollow in the gloom of the corridor. "You're leaving again, aren't you?" she said.

"We have to spread out the search. I'll be more useful out there than in here."

"I want to come with you," she said.

"No," he said. "You have to stay. If Benjamin tries to contact us in any way, it will be through you, and it will be here." He slipped his feet into his hiking boots.

"At least tell me where you're going!" she insisted.

"To recover the spaceship," he said.

She gasped, then grasped his arm. "You're

going to the Canary Islands, aren't you?"

He glanced at her without answering.

"Mesmo, please! I need to come!"

He bent to tie his shoelaces and shook his head. "No," he repeated. Seeing the look on her face, he added, "I know this is hard, but we have to split up our efforts. I'll cover a lot more ground with the spaceship. And I need you here, centralizing the information. Let me know as soon as Inspector Hao uncovers any new leads. Will you do that for me?"

Her face contorted in anguish, and she opened her mouth to argue, then paused and nodded instead. "Fine," she said. "But... just wait for a second, will you? Don't go yet." She turned and disappeared into the living-room.

Mesmo continued lacing his boots, glancing up as he wondered what she was doing.

She hurried back, holding up a backpack against her chest as she struggled to put a reusable waterbottle in it. She dropped the backpack in his arms and zipped up the top. "It's just some food rations, water, a flashlight, and..." She held up his smartphone. "...you were going to forget this."

He took the smartphone from her, smiling, then swung the backpack over his shoulder.

She rubbed her forearms as she looked at

him, her face downcast. "At least I felt useful for a minute."

He took her by the shoulders and pulled her into an embrace. "Benjamin needs you to be strong right now," he said. "*I* need you to be strong."

She was silent for a moment, then breathed, "It's just that, I can't lose you, too."

Mesmo held her tight and sucked in air. "You won't," he said, then looked at her with determination. "And I'll find Benjamin, I promise."

He kissed her, then let himself out of the house into a grey drizzle. Watching her frail form in the doorway as he jogged away from the house, he knew there was no way he could have told her about the danger he was about to get himself into.

* * *

Full of renewed determination, Ben entered what he found to be an incredibly well-maintained stable. A couple of curious horses came to check him out, but most were busy munching at their breakfast. Ben admired the beautiful steeds, aware that these must indeed be horses of the highest breed. Some were black, some brown, others, white. They held their refined heads high, pawing at the ground as they sensed his skill.

Most did not pay much attention to him, however. He was not someone who wielded a power to be contended with. He did not have a whip to order them to attention, or fresh dates to seduce them. They did, however, make it clear that they did not know the horse Sadalbari.

Disappointed, Ben turned to head out again, when the trainer entered the stables and led the purebred to its stall without noticing him. Ben approached silently, not wanting to startle the horse or trainer, and watched as the man bent to plunge a thick brush into a bucket of water, then, with his back turned to Ben, gently and purposefully began scrubbing the horse's back. The horse neighed with pleasure, shaking its long mane, and Ben found himself fascinated with the way the trainer scrubbed in a slow, patient way as if he were accomplishing the most important task of the day.

Wouldn't mind a scrub, myself.

A chestnut coloured horse nudged its muzzle Ben's way from the neighbouring stall. It did not look the same as the others. It was smaller, with a long, flaxen mane and tail.

Ben rubbed its muzzle. *You are different from the others.*

I could say the same for you. What is your name?

I am Benjamin Archer. What is yours?

It is Nutmeg.

Ben smiled. *That's a good name.*

Thank you. I have never seen you before. You are new here. Where do you come from?

A fleeting image of rolling hills and tall cornfields flashed through Ben's mind before he could stop himself.

Nutmeg snorted in surprise. *My home was like that, too.*

Ben gasped as Nutmeg showed him green pastures and apple trees. The horse sent him a deep sense of longing.

You miss it!

Nutmeg shook her mane. *Yes, even after all these years. I am treated well here, but I still long for green grass.*

Ben turned and found the trainer staring at him. The man wore a beige tunic and headdress, and a neatly trimmed beard like the other men on the property. His face was kindly, not surly like the Sheikh's.

He smiled at Ben and invited him to enter

Nutmeg's stall. Then he fetched another bucket, which he filled with water and brought to Ben's side. Still smiling, he placed a similar brush in Ben's hand and indicated he should dip it in the bucket. Ben obliged and began scrubbing Nutmeg's mane.

The man watched him, then shook his head, took the brush from him and showed him how to scrub: slowly, gently, up and down, as if he were painting. He handed the brush back to Ben and nodded encouragingly. Ben tried again.

Ah, yes! That feels good! Nutmeg snorted in contentment, making Ben grin.

The trainer's eyes twinkled as he went back to his own labour.

Ben scrubbed and scrubbed as if in a trance, relieved to have found something else to think about—until his chaperone appeared at the entrance of the stables, reminding him of his plight. The trainer and the chaperone exchanged a few words. The chaperone hesitated for a brief moment, then left, shooting a glance Ben's way that said, "Don't you dare try anything funny."

Ben shivered, but as he went back to scrubbing, he felt a weight lift from his shoulders. It wasn't that the chaperone treated him unkindly. On the contrary, he had so far shown only worry for Ben's wellbeing, but Ben couldn't help it. Without the chaperone, he felt slightly less like a prisoner.

The trainer placed his hand on Ben's arm to indicate he should stop scrubbing, then took his bucket and led him to a hand-operated water pump. Ben washed his hands under the cool liquid and found blisters forming.

The trainer noticed. He took a towel and gently pressed it on Ben's hands to dry them, as if Ben now required his full attention, the way he had given it to the horse. Ben was surprised to find the man's hands were strong without being cracked or hard from labouring with the horses.

The man placed his hand on his heart and said, "Hakim."

Ben did the same and said, "Ben."

Hakim gave him a radiant smile, then seemed to think of something. He gestured for Ben to follow him. Hakim led Ben away from the training area and up the stairs, all the way to the main entrance, then on to the side of the property that Ben hadn't finished exploring yet.

This side of the property was quieter. Fewer people bustled about. The area felt newer and more modern, and Ben guessed these were the sleeping quarters of the property's owners. They came near to the end of a long corridor and passed through some archways onto a wider patio than the ones Ben had seen so far.

He stopped and saw a pool. Dug into the middle of the adobe patio, it gurgled at the far end as the surface cascaded over the border into a lush garden of flowery bushes and palm trees that descended to the ground level.

On his left stood a square tent with a burgundy carpet underneath. Red-and-gold cushions lay around it and, in the middle, a very large, golden platter with an intricate, golden tea-set. The whole thing created a peaceful, refreshing atmosphere, and Ben wished circumstances had been different so that he could have laid back and enjoyed the view of the dunes.

Hakim must have read his mind because he nodded Ben's way, gesturing that he should use the pool.

Ben's eyes widened. What would the Sheikh think if he saw him using his private swimming pool? And, anyway, the pool was so clean and pure, it looked more like an architectural decoration than an actual pool.

Hakim yelled something at a man who was sweeping the floor nearby. The man sped away, then returned with swim trunks and a couple of plush towels. Ben received the items, completely stunned.

It was as if he'd landed in a private, exclusive resort, which clashed in his mind with what he'd experienced so far.

Hakim smiled and nodded at the items, then turned and left without a word. Ben stared after him, then at the swimming pool.

By now, the harsh sun had risen high in the sky, and Ben's hoodie, which he had refused to take off so far in the slim hope he would suddenly be whisked home, was suffocating.

The servant who had brought the items disappeared, and Ben was left in front of this idyllic spot as if he were the grand master of a palace.

He stood there for a long moment, a painful lump forming in his throat.

There was something about the serene view, the bubbling water and chirping birds that made him want to scream. He was supposed to be home, planning his and Mesmo's mission, finding support among world leaders to help in the plight faced by the living creatures that inhabited the Earth. Every minute he stood there, more animals could be dying. Instead, he was stuck here, in the middle of nowhere, waiting. *Forced* to wait.

Boiling anger rose to his cheeks. Only, there was no-one to vent his frustration on. He fought back tears and remembered he was supposed to think rationally. He found a men's room located right next to the swimming pool, changed irritably, and dipped his toes into the refreshing water. The welcoming coolness came as such a shock, he almost sobbed. It was easy, then, to slip into the water and let himself sink to the bottom. He opened his eyes and watched the sunlight caress the pool's surface, listening only to his heartbeat.

The water reminded him of Mesmo. What were Mesmo and his mom doing now? They must be sick with worry. Would they involve the police?

And his captors: on the one hand. they treated him like a noble guest, but on the other hand, they made it clear he was not to stray beyond certain borders.

Overwhelmed by feelings of helplessness, he shut his eyes and let out the long, muffled scream he had been holding in.

CHAPTER 10 *A Place in Africa*

Time ceased to exist. Ben must have spent hours in the pool, whiling the minutes away as he tried to come up with an escape plan. He stepped out once his wrinkled fingers looked like they belonged to an old man. He plodded to the tent, wrapped himself in a towel, and sank onto the luxurious carpet and cushions. A hot breeze made the palm trees sway and lulled him into a deep, unplanned sleep.

The call to prayer woke him, just as the sun touched the dunes in a fiery ball. Once again, a well-laden tray of food had been placed on a low table next to Ben.

He sat up and discovered his jeans, shirt and hoodie beside it. He unfolded them. They had been washed, dried, and the hole in his hoodie had been sown together.

This made Ben so furious he kicked at the golden platter in the middle of the tent, sending the tea set flying. The pieces clattered loudly to the ground.

Did they think a fancy meal and a sewn hoodie would soothe his aching heart? Or make him more compliant? How could this have happened? How could he be stuck here, completely helpless, lost to the world like a grain of sand on these endless dunes? Frustration consumed him.

He had things to do, projects to accomplish. He was supposed to be packing for his trip to Canmore, working on his website with his friends, planning for The Great Gathering in Brazil. Instead, he was stuck in a timeless place, for the sole pleasure of a spoiled child.

He put on his shirt gruffly, pacing the pool's edge in a useless attempt to calm himself. That morning, he'd found a source of energy and hope within himself. Now, that hope had vanished into the pit of his stomach, far from his reach.

The sound of distant neighing pulled him out of his dark thoughts. He shaded his eyes and spotted Hakim carrying a heavy bulk of straw in the distance. The poor man was still working away, he realized. His anger ebbed and was replaced by a sense of guilt. Here he was, feeling sorry for himself, resting next to a luxurious swimming pool with all the food he could eat, while Hakim hadn't stopped working all afternoon.

He looked at the food tray, then bit his lip, a sudden idea crossing his mind.

After dressing in a hurry, Ben picked up the tray and carried it all the way to the stables. He was afraid Hakim would be gone by the time he arrived, but he found the horse trainer closing up for the night. The man's movements were still as meticulous and flowing as they had been that morning, and Ben realized how soothing his calm manners must be to the horses.

The trainer turned and noticed Ben.

Ben showed him the food tray. "Um, I thought you might be hungry?" He felt extremely shy, unsure of what was considered polite or impolite in this country.

Hakim smiled his usual calm smile. He shut the door, then placed a hand on Ben's shoulder and led him to the side of the stables. A set of stairs climbed along the outside of the building and led to its roof. The roof was flat, and Hakim sat on its edge, inviting Ben to join him.

Ben caught his breath. It was one of the best outlooks on the property. Buildings stretched out to his right: some houses, the main building, then the Sheikh's living quarters with the swimming pool at the end. The adobe wall surrounded most of the property, except where there were openings and terraces leading to the green oasis. Beyond all of this was a sea of high dunes, with a sliver of the blood-red sun still clinging to the horizon.

Ben spotted a lonely road leading away from the property by the main entrance, cutting through the desert. Where it went to was left to his wildest guess.

Dusk fell, hanging lights came on around the buildings, and a fire was lit by the oasis. Dark shadows of camels cut out against the starry sky, and Ben swallowed this remarkable view with his eyes as he munched on some flat-bread.

Hakim ate his share, always making sure Ben ate his part first and pointed to various foods on the well-laden tray: cardamom tea, khameer, biseetah, beriani... Ben practiced saying the words, welcoming the company of somebody who so far had not threatened him.

Darkness fell, and bright stars came out over the desert. Yet, in the distance, Ben noticed a splash of misty light that could not have come from the setting sun. He pointed to it and said, "Hakim, what's that?"

Hakim followed his finger and nodded. "Dubai," he said.

Ben gawked. *"Dubai?"* His mind did a double flip. He knew about Dubai. He had mentioned it to Mesmo, during their long hours together looking at the world map, studying famous landmarks and major cities.

Dubai! That was an ultra-modern city with skyscrapers that touched the sky and man-made islands filled with top-notch hotels. Ben pictured a gleaming city teeming with life and happy tourists spending wads of dollar bills.

His heart yearned for contact with the outside world. It was just there, out of reach. He imagined himself taking one giant leap from the rooftop into the city.

Stupid, of course.

His throat dried as his previous theory of being stuck in the middle of the Sahara Desert toppled to the ground. Dubai was not in Africa, but somewhere in the Middle East, if he remembered correctly. There was something satisfying about being able to place himself on the world map again, but also a mountain-load of questions as to what to do next.

At least now he knew where the road in front of the property went. His mind reeled with a jumble of calculations as he wondered whether he could make it to Dubai on foot...

"Sadalbari," Hakim said, startling Ben out of his feverish thoughts.

Ben turned to Hakim and found the man looking up at the night sky. Ben frowned, confused. "Did you say Sadalbari?"

Hakim nodded. "Sadalbari," he repeated. He saw the question-mark on Ben's face and smiled. He moved the tray to make some space between them and, with his index finger, drew several dots in the thin layer of sand that covered the roof. He joined the dots and gestured to the whole drawing. "Um..." he searched for the words, "Constellation. In your culture: Pegasus. Winged Horse." He then pointed at a particular area in the sky and said, "In my culture: Sadalbari. The Splendid One."

Ben gaped at the rough sketch, then up at the stars. He saw Hakim's drawing reflected there. "Wow!" he breathed. "I thought Sadalbari was just the name of the Sheik's horse?"

Hakim stared at the stars. "Sadalbari new horse of Sheikh Azhar bin-Rahman and son, Zayed." His face fell for the first time, making a disturbing idea blossom in Ben's mind.

"You are very good with horses," he noted. "Have *you* tried training Sadalbari?"

Hakim didn't answer, and Ben didn't know if he had understood him or not. Or maybe he didn't want to answer. But his silence proved that the man had heard of the newly acquired steed.

Hakim stood suddenly, brushing the sand from his tunic.

Ben straightened. "Where are you going?"

"Home," Hakim smiled, his previous down-turned face brightening. "To wife and seven children."

"You have seven children?" Ben gasped. His heart squeezed painfully, realizing people here went home to their families once their workday was over.

Hakim's eyes twinkled. "Seven splendid ones. My constellation," he said, then placed his hand over his heart. "Thank you for sharing your food. *Assalamu alaikum*[4], Ben," he said, before slipping into the night.

Ben dropped onto his back, loneliness rolling over him in waves. He tried to focus on

---

[4] *Assalamu alaikum* = Arabic farewell greeting meaning "Peace be upon you".

Hakim. The poor man spent his whole day doing hard labour with the horses, probably trying to make ends meet so he could feed his large family. All this while some rich child hopped from one luxurious location to the next, playing with his new toys along the way.

A satellite flickered across the star-filled sky. Ben followed its arched path as it curved around the Earth. He stretched his hand as if to touch it, imagining it was Mesmo searching for him in his spaceship.

* * *

Mesmo didn't go to the Canary Islands.

Perhaps Ben had been there, briefly, but Mesmo was convinced he wouldn't find answers on the Spanish islands. He needed to go beyond.

Ben's trace had gone cold off the coast of Northern Africa. Curiously, Akeya *was* from Africa—from Kenya, to be exact. And the fact that she, too, had disappeared, made Mesmo want to get there as fast as possible. Perhaps the breadcrumbs he was following were not breadcrumbs at all. Maybe he was creating a theory in his mind out of his desperation to find Ben, but it was not lost to him that a plane could easily have flown from the Canary Islands to Kenya.

With that in mind, he raced over miles of Saharan Desert, then veered to the South until he reached Kenya. He landed the spaceship near a group of acacia trees and walked across the dry African grasslands to Akeya's small village.

He entered the red, dusty street bordered by round huts made from tree branches and cow dung. The silence in the village made Mesmo slow down. It had not been like this the last time he had come.

When he had travelled to Kenya many months before, smiling children had run to greet him. They had led him excitedly to Akeya's hut. There, she had invited him to share a meal before handing him one of the seven Toreq keys, which she had filled with thorough, hard-earned information about the region. The meeting had been warm and generous.

Now, fear hung over the village.

A movement caught Mesmo's eye. There, behind a tree, a child was peeking at him.

He recognized the little girl. He had seen her the last time, too. She had laughed at him, her dark eyes twinkling at the prospect of showing a visitor around her village. Now, she pulled at her lip, hesitating to come forward from behind the tree.

Mesmo crouched down so he wouldn't look imposing, something he knew tended to happen because of his height.

She seemed to recognize him because she ran forward to meet him. She grabbed his hand and pulled him after her, eyes wide, face unsmiling. She brought him to Akeya's hut, which he found empty.

He stared questioningly at the little girl. She pointed to an acacia tree not far from Akeya's home. Mesmo followed her direction, approaching the tree with care.

And then he saw it—the grave.

He bent next to it and stared at the little girl, who pulled at her lip again with big, sad eyes. Other villagers approached, having recognized him from his previous visit. Some wept, others called Akeya's name as if wanting to call her forth from beyond. Mesmo rubbed his face with his hands, a terrible heaviness falling over his heart.

Akeya, dead! Su Tai, dead!

Honourable Wise Ones, who had stood by his and Ben's side in their efforts to teach humans to lead a more balanced life. Had their decision to help him led to a death sentence?

Two Wise Ones lost in the space of a week. And Ben, gone! This couldn't be a coincidence, could it?

And the constant appearances of UFOs in various parts of the world that Amaru had pointed out to him on social media—that couldn't be a coincidence either, could it?

He placed his hand on the acacia tree, his skill emanating through his palm, and called forth the tree's water. The clear liquid seeped onto the ground in tiny rivulets that shone like liquid silver, and he turned them into a beautiful, delicate ice-design over Akeya's grave.

He sat there, watching over the Wise One's last resting place, feeling the tentacles of a major trap closing in on him. And he knew—as he had suspected from the very beginning—that it was time for him to pay Einar a visit.

CHAPTER 11 *Bird's-Eye View*

Ben hurried to the stables the next morning, but Hakim was not there. Disappointed, he went to greet Nutmeg, who told him Hakim only came once a week.

Nutmeg must have sensed his sadness because she nudged Ben and asked to be taken outside for a ride.

Ben hesitated. *I've never ridden a horse before!*

I will show you.

Ben looked for riding gear, but Nutmeg stopped him. *You don't need it; follow my instructions.*

Ben did as he was told, opened the gate so Nutmeg could come out, and followed the horse into the clearing. Nutmeg went to stand beside a fence and told Ben to use it so he could reach the horse's back more easily. Ben did so, swung his leg over the horse and found himself balancing precariously on the slippery back.

Hold on to my mane.

Ben grabbed the horse's long, pallid hair urgently, making Nutmeg snort.

Don't be so nervous! I'll be gentle, I promise.
I... I think I'm going to slip off.

Ben had barely uttered the thought when he lost his balance and ended in a heap on the ground.

Nutmeg pawed happily and insisted: *Again!*

Ben stood and clapped his hands together to get rid of the sand, then climbed on to Nutmeg's back again. This time they made it to the middle of the training area before he slipped off again.

Nutmeg pranced around him, full of excitement. *Again!*

Determined, Ben climbed on the horse's back.

Nutmeg made a huge effort to walk at a slow pace. *They do not ride me often. The other Arabian horses are prized above me. I am of no use to them now.*

Ben gave his new friend a comforting tap on

the neck, before grasping a handful of hair as he wobbled. He straightened himself, then loosened his grip, clearing his throat. *Why are you here, then?*

As soon as he asked the question, Ben knew the answer. *Were you Zayed's horse?*

Nutmeg did not answer right away. *I was his horse, yes, when he first learned to ride.*

Ben thought Nutmeg didn't want to say any more, but then the horse's words chilled him.

Zayed is no good. Stay away from him.

They had left the training area by now and were heading away from the protective walls of the property towards the fresh oasis nestled at the bottom of the dunes.

Ben had never been this far before, and when he checked the buildings, he was quick to notice his chaperone, who followed his every move from one of the rooftops.

Nutmeg, let's get out of here, you and me!

The horse snorted. *That's not possible. There is only death outside this estate.*

But what about the road? It leads to Dubai. We could follow it and find help.

Nutmeg flickered her ears. *Even in a straight line, I believe it is too far. You should ask the falcon.*

Ben blinked. *The falcon?* He looked up automatically, squinting, and found the falcon flying in circles high above him. His heart leapt. He slid off the horse's back, climbed the nearest dune, then asked the falcon for permission to fly with her. The falcon agreed.

Ben's thoughts lifted from the ground and entered the bird's body. Strong wings lifted him on an invisible flow of hot air, and he watched with glee as the Sheik's property became smaller and smaller below him. He rested his mind on the bird's back, enjoying the liberating sensation of flying. He observed the vast landscape through the bird's sharp eyes, noticing a scurrying mouse in the sand, the winding traces left by a snake, the straight road that left the property. He followed it on and on from within the bird's mind, becoming ever more discouraged at its seemingly endless length until the falcon's eyes captured the skyline of one of the world's most modern cities.

But it's so far!

The falcon agreed. *It is a day's flight away. Two days on horseback, at least.*

Crestfallen, Ben was about to let go of the falcon when something glimmered to his right. The falcon glided in that direction, and Ben watched a convoy of black cars slide along the road. One of them being a long limousine. His mind whirled. *The Sheik's son!*

Nutmeg neighed in a far corner of his mind. The falcon swooped down, letting Ben slip back into his body. He opened his eyes. His chaperone stood over him, reaching out to grab him.

Nutmeg reared. The falcon flapped its wings a few inches from the man's head, making him hunch back in terror.

"Stop!" Ben ordered, holding out his hands to calm the animals. *It's okay,* he reassured them. *Don't hurt him.*

Nutmeg huffed and calmed down, while the falcon took to the skies again.

The man wiped away the sweat from his brow, fear reflected in his eyes as he stared at Ben. Staying at a safe distance, the chaperone pointed pleadingly at the estate and said a single word, "Master!"

CHAPTER 12 *Sadalbari*

By the time Ben had finished taking Nutmeg back to the stables and reached the main entrance, people were still pouring out of the convoy. The lobby bustled with activity. There were suitcases and boxes everywhere. A string of servants whisked some of them away, and yet still there were more littering the floor.

Ben hopped over them, his chaperone in tow, and followed the flow of people who came and went from the right wing of the property. Ben's stride increased, as did his heartbeat. It seemed the Sheikh's son had decided to arrive several days earlier than planned, which suited him fine. At last! He was going to give this Zayed a piece of his mind.

Suitcases were being dropped off in a room bordered by a terrace, but when Ben tried to enter, a bodyguard appeared out of nowhere, blocking his passage. Ben jumped back, his skin crawling. It was one of the men who had kidnapped him, he was sure of it. Stomach twisting, he pulled back and paced before the room, eyeing the bodyguard warily, but also hoping to catch a glimpse of Zayed.

Steaming food was brought into the room. The comings-and-goings of busy servants slowed down to a trickle, and with each passing minute, Ben became more and more frustrated.

What's taking so long?

He needed things to get done. He needed to clear up his situation. He needed to know when he was going home.

He spotted his chaperone and asked, "Sadalbari? Zayed?"

The man shook his head. He placed his hands under his ear and closed his eyes to indicate that Zayed was sleeping, then pointed at Ben to suggest he do the same.

Fire smouldered in Ben's stomach. *The poor boy's sleeping, is he?*

"Then wake him up!" he yelled, startling the man, who made a hurried gesture to keep silent.

"What?" Ben yelled. "Is daddy's boy tired? Does he need a nap? Did he have too much vacation? You will take me to him, right now!"

He couldn't stop shouting. It was as if a dam broke inside of him, and he couldn't stop the flow of words.

His chaperone looked terrified, and rightly so because the bodyguard picked up Ben and dragged him into his own bedroom. He shoved Ben inside and closed the door, locking it.

Ben was so furious he kicked at it multiple times, not really believing it would open, but because he needed to vent his frustration.

As day turned into night, Ben continued to pace around the room, his brain working like a locomotive letting off too much steam. It was exhausting, this roller-coaster of emotions. One moment things were finally happening, and the next, he was drowning in despair.

He must have paced several miles around the room before he managed to calm down. His mother's voice came through to him, settling his thoughts and feelings of desperation. She was telling him to take a deep breath and think.

He placed his head in his hands and stared at the floor. A corner of his single black sneaker stuck out from under the upholstered bench.

Hand trembling, Ben picked it up and turned it over. Dry mud still stuck to it from his hike with Mesmo.

Ben scrubbed at the dirt, tears welling behind his eyes. He'd meant to clean the sneakers so his mom wouldn't get mad at him for leaving muddy footprints in the house.

"Mesmo, what should I do?" he breathed.

He was still staring at the sneaker when his chaperone tiptoed into the room, casting a nervous glance his way. The man dropped off a tray with the evening meal, then tiptoed out again.

Ben sat at the edge of the bed with his feet resting on the bench. He remained there for most of the night, thinking. He didn't touch the food and slept little.

But by dawn, he was resolute.

There was no way around it: no matter how much he hated the idea, he would have to do the Sheikh's bidding. It was his only way out. He thought about it over and over and always came back to the same conclusion. He wanted to go home, but that would never happen if he kept on fighting his captors. He was one against many and did not stand a chance. His only hope of going home was to suppress his feelings of anger and pride and get the boy on his horse.

Several times during the night, he'd imagined turning Sadalbari to his favour, jumping on the horse's back and fleeing into the dunes. Or maybe he could release all the Arabian horses and cause havoc on the property. His restless mind also imagined slipping into the trunk of the limousine, or one of the other cars. Lastly, he thought about asking Hakim for help. But that somehow felt unfair. The man had seven children; he couldn't risk losing his job because of Ben.

On and on, Ben's thoughts went, with his mother's voice always returning him to a more balanced place.

When his chaperone entered the next morning and said, "Sadalbari," Ben was ready.

He nodded, calmly ate everything the man had brought him, showered, and this time put on the tunic that still lay on the upholstered bench. The cotton fabric was light and soft—way more comfortable than his Western styled clothes, which were not adapted to the desert climate.

His chaperone beamed at the result, and Ben wondered if the man was scolded every time Ben didn't do as he was told. He realized he didn't even know the man's name.

Copying the horse trainer, he put his hand over his heart and said, "Ben."

The man's face shone. He gave a short bow and said, "Abdul."

Ben nodded. "Thanks, Abdul."

They were about to leave the room when, on a hunch, Ben doubled back and grabbed four sugar-cubes from the food-tray and stuffed them in his pocket.

The place was bustling. Was it because of Zayed and Sadalbari?

Ben gritted his teeth, thinking back on his TV appearance. *They want a circus stunt? I'll give them a circus stunt!*

"Just do it and come home, Ben," his mother's voice whispered in his mind.

Determined, Ben walked to the training area where several people had gathered in excited anticipation. He was led to the center of the arena, noticing how everyone else stood or sat behind the fence surrounding it. The attention he was getting led to a fluttery feeling in his stomach. This was a bigger deal than he had expected. Was it really necessary for half of the property's inhabitants to come and watch daddy's boy ride his new horse?

Murmurs around the ring made Ben turn, and he discovered a group of men walking towards an elevated platform with lavish chairs and cushions on them.

A teenager took a seat in the central chair.

A... teenager?

Ben stared. Was this Zayed, the Sheikh's son? All along, he had expected a young boy—younger than him, at least. But this guy must have been sixteen or seventeen.

Ben couldn't help staring, and his blood began to boil again when he saw Zayed lean back into the chair in a bored manner, the way the Sheikh had done not long ago. The teen stared at his smartphone, ignoring his neighbours who tried to chat with him.

He doesn't even care!

The realization struck Ben. He was just another toy in Zayed's collection, a brief entertainment until a new toy came along. Balling his fists, he was about to lose control of his temper when something new began to happen. Zayed sensed it too because he dropped the phone and leaned forward, showing interest in the arena for the first time.

A truck pulled out into the open space.

Ben turned to face it. The truck's motor died, and silence fell over the spectators. But Ben had already forgotten about them. The hairs on the back of his head prickled, and his brow began to sweat. Horses in the stables neighed, sending waves of worry his way.

Blood raged through Ben's ears. The alien skill woke within him like lightning bolts. A powerful presence filled his mind, and Ben knew even before the truck door opened that Sadalbari was inside.

Deep thuds coming from within the truck echoed through the arena, sending ripples of awe from the spectators. And Ben realized that something was terribly, terribly wrong.

The back of the truck flew open, revealing only shadows, like the mouth of a cavern hiding a fiery dragon. The beast breathed within.

A moment that lasted a heartbeat passed, and then Sadalbari emerged. The finest of stallions. Stunning. With a pure-white coat and flowing mane. It stepped out into the sunlight like a magical creature from another realm.

It stopped at the edge of the arena; calculating, brilliant, and unreal—casting its dominant presence over everyone. It snorted like a locomotive, slow and purposeful. Its voice blasting into Ben's mind. *Move over, Fly, or I will crush you.*

Nutmeg whinnied in terror from within the stables. *Run, Benjamin!*

Ben couldn't find his legs. Never in a million years would it have occurred to him that Sadalbari was a king of horses, a steed that called on you to kneel.

A wild soul. That's what the Sheikh's interpreter had said. The understatement of the century. Never, not ever in a million years, would Sadalbari allow anyone to touch it, let alone mount it.

The stallion huffed from the other side of the arena, its fiery eyes set on Ben, and it took just a single powerful image for Ben to understand he would not live to see the end of the day.

CHAPTER 13 *Zayed*

Never in his life had Ben encountered such a powerful creature.

Sure, there were the predators—be they mere alley cats or white sharks. These creatures, though, were spurred on by a natural instinct to survive, ingrained in their subconscious since the beginning of time.

This was different.

Sadalbari was an Emperor of horses, a King of Kings, wild to the core. He trotted imposingly at the edge of the arena, calculating, planning, savouring the moment before he galloped across it to smother Ben.

He glanced rapidly at Zayed and found the teen bending forward in his seat, eyes glued on the horse.

Enjoying the show...

Sadalbari stopped pacing and stared at Ben, its tail of pure-white flicking. It did not need to speak. Its mere aura told Ben to scram, but Ben found himself rooted to the spot, cold sweat dripping down his back. The sugar cubes he had brought to befriend the horse slid out of his hand, forgotten.

The stallion moved forward at a slow, deliberate pace, and all Ben could mutter was, "Oh, crap!"

Sadalbari picked up speed and made ready to trample Ben to the ground. He lifted his hands in desperation. *No. STOP!* His own voice boomed in his head.

Sadalbari retreated a few steps, intrigued.

Ben heard a tiny wave of wonder among the crowd, but that only ignited the stallion's anger. This time it lunged, shoving Ben aside with its shoulder and sending him sprawling onto his back.

It bellowed, *What are you, creature?*

I am Benjamin Archer. I know you can hear me. I wish to speak with you!

You may not! I am Sadalbari, King of the Desert. I decide who speaks and who dies. You bother me, Fly.

Ben jumped to his feet, preparing for another assault.

Wait! Noble One, will you kill the messenger before you hear the message?

Sadalbari followed Ben's every move, nostrils inches from his face. Ben knew he was just toying with him.

Speak, then, Fly.

The horse dared him to speak, but Ben knew it was at his own peril. He had no choice but to try, so he pointed at Zayed and tapped into the horse's arrogance.

The young subject, on the chair there, has dared to request your Highness allow him permission to mount on your back.

Sadalbari stared at Ben, then at Zayed. A hollow, cruel laugh escaped its steaming muzzle, making Ben's skin crawl.

Do you not think I know that, Fly? Do you not think he has already tried? Perhaps he has forgotten what happened the last time. Shall I remind him?

Sadalbari took a step back and reared. The last thing Ben saw were hooves crashing down on him.

* * *

Shouts came from every corner. Arms dragged Ben away.

Sadalbari screamed, sending thoughts as sharp as knives into Ben's mind.

Ben blinked and watched people run chaotically around him. A searing pain ran up his arm. He clenched his teeth and tried to sit up.

Out of the corner of his eye, he caught Zayed walking away. The show had ended, the curtains had dropped, and there was nothing left to see.

It took six strong men with lassos to pin down Sadalbari, who neighed in rage.

Abdul brought an ice pack and gently rolled up Ben's sleeve. The man's exclamation made Ben turn away from the pureblood and look at his arm. A burning red welt, the shape of a half-moon, throbbed angrily at him.

Abdul covered it with the ice pack, and Ben bit his tongue at the pain. Then he focused again on Sadalbari, who was being dragged into the stables. Even the Arabian horses did not agree with the stallion joining them. Ben could hear them stomping and snorting in protest in their stalls.

Ben sat, stunned by the encounter. Never once had it occurred to him that Sadalbari would have been unapproachable. Getting Zayed on to the horse's back was now out of the question. He could not do what needed to be done, so that the Sheikh could send him home.

His dismay turned to anger. This was all Zayed's fault. How could the teenager have put him in harm's way like that? He shoved Abdul's hand away, stood a bit too quickly, then had to grab on to Abdul's shoulder when his head swayed. Abdul wanted to help him, but Ben would have none of it.

I've had enough of this!

He marched in the direction the teenager had gone and searched the main entrance, then the corridors. He found the Sheikh's son at the edge of the swimming pool, taking off a bathing robe and entering the clear blue water, where he dropped his sunglasses over his eyes. A servant handed him a fresh-pressed juice brimming with ice and topped with a straw.

Burly men stepped in front of Ben, cutting off his intense strides toward the pool.

"Hey! I need to talk to you!" Ben yelled, trying to get around them.

Zayed gestured to let him through.

Ben ignored the bodyguards and stomped to the edge of the pool. "Did you enjoy the show?" he yelled.

Zayed sipped at his straw. "Hello to you too, horse whisperer." He had not yet grown a beard, and his skin was a golden almond colour, fit for the unforgiving sun. He had a flawless British accent.

Ben seethed. "You knew Sadalbari couldn't be trusted. But you sent me to face him anyway. Do you realize I could have been killed?"

Zayed stared at him through his dark sunglasses. "I was not worried. The media spoke highly of your abilities." He paused. "Or should I consider, then, that they stretched the truth?" He let the question hang.

Ben's emotions boiled over. "This has nothing to do with my abilities. That horse has lost a screw. He's crazy! There's no way you're ever going to ride him." He marched back and forth, then added. "I've had enough of this. You're sending me home right now, do you understand?"

The shadow of a smirk appeared at the corner of Zayed's mouth. "Or what, whisperer?" he said in a low voice, putting aside his drink and sunglasses.

Ben tensed like an icepick. "You have no

right to hold me here against my will."

Zayed did not hear him; he had slipped under the water, forcing Ben to wait until he resurfaced. Zayed shook his wet hair, spraying drops of water around him, then rested his arm along Ben's side of the pool. "My father gave me a gift: the mightiest stallion the world has ever seen. Do you have any idea about the value of this beast? How hard it was to catch him? You don't realize how privileged you are to be working with such a legendary specimen."

Ben gritted his teeth. "I told you: he cannot be mounted. He won't listen."

Zayed swam backwards to the spot where he had left his drink, then shrugged. "If he does not listen, then break him."

He spoke the words in such a natural tone that Ben had to think for a second before they sank in.

Break him.

Was Zayed suggesting Ben take over the horse's mind and break his spirit? Mesmo's voice echoed in his ears, "Using the skill to take over another living being's spirit is against the Toreq law, and punishable by death."

"You're as crazy as Sadalbari," Ben gasped, realizing how far the teenager would go to get

what he wanted.

"Watch your mouth, whisperer," Zayed snarled.

Ben stood his ground. He locked eyes with Zayed and said purposefully, "What was it that happened the last time you tried to ride Sadalbari?"

Zayed tensed, the straw half-way to his mouth. He covered his eyes with his sunglasses, his face expressionless, but his words were as cold as the ice cubes in his drink. "You should get to work, whisperer, or you'll be stuck here for a very long time." He gestured to his fridge-sized bodyguards, who were at Ben's side in a blink. They grabbed him by each arm and pulled him back into the corridor.

Ben winced as they pressed on his wound but could not find his voice to protest. His only worth was the task he had been appointed with and which he now knew he could not deliver.

Dumbfounded, Ben slid into a sitting position against the wall of the corridor and grabbed his hair with his hands. Today was supposed to be the day he accomplished the Sheikh's wishes, and the Sheikh would send him home. Now he was stuck with a sore arm, a crazy horse, and an arrogant teenager who thought he owned the world.

CHAPTER 14 *Mirage*

You'll be stuck here for a very long time, Zayed had said. Ben's heart sank to the bottom of his feet. *A very long time.* The words repeated in his head, like a hurricane ploughing through his mind. He stood, placing one foot before the other, *long time, long time,* his brain said with each step.

He reached the entrance hallway, at a loss as to what to think or what to do when his eyes fell on a table against the wall. A crisp newspaper lay on it, sprawled with words from the Arabic alphabet. His eyes fell on the one printed thing that he understood: the date.

"October 15th," Ben read.

Canadian Thanksgiving Day. Today was the day he was supposed to be in Canmore, celebrating Thanksgiving with his mother and friends.

He swayed on his feet and had to hang on to the side of the table. With everything going on, he had somehow lost track of the days, stupidly convincing himself that this nightmare would be over by the time Thanksgiving came. And now Thanksgiving had come and gone, and he could never bring it back.

He stared at the front door. It was ajar. There wasn't a single guard in sight. His feet took him towards it. He opened the door, passed through it, and found himself in a large, circular driveway in the beating sun.

He walked on as if in a trance, breathing hard, expecting to be held back at any moment. But he no longer cared. He crossed the paved area, passed by the fountain in the middle, the golden gates to the estate, then ended up on the asphalt of the single road that led to Dubai.

The sun struck the black surface, heat pounding down from above and below, and Ben stared at the end of the road that disappeared into a hazy swelter. His mountain-hike with Mesmo was long gone, his plans for The Great Gathering a distant memory. His mother and Kimi were like a fading dream. The tears did not have time to reach his cheeks, evaporating the minute they left his eyes.

He walked on. No-one noticed. No-one cared.

He stopped and stared at the road floating into nothingness. He waited—hoping for a sign, a glimmer of hope. A spot moved in his direction through the waves of heat.

Ben stared, confused. The spot turned into a hazy shadow, then into a person—a man with white hair. Ben's mouth fell open, certain that his eyes were playing tricks on him. His heart beat faster. "Mesmo?" he gasped.

By what miracle...?

The mirage turned into a solid person, but the man did not have white hair. He wore a white tunic and a white headdress.

Hakim.

The trainer opened his arms as he approached, and Ben let himself sink into his embrace. Hakim held him in the middle of the furnace, silent but genuine.

"I can't do it," Ben said, realizing his defeat. "I can't get out. I... I don't know what to do."

Hakim didn't say a word. He led Ben back down the road, through the gates, past the driveway, and into the coolness of the main entrance.

Ben didn't realize until now how dangerous it was outside. A few minutes longer on the black asphalt, and he might as well have been toast. Hakim placed a glass of water in his hand, which he gulped down. The water slid into every limb, and they screamed for more.

The horse trainer continued to lead him away, outside again, down some steps, out into the sand, then under the shade of the palm trees of the small oasis. High overhead, the falcon screeched as it flew in circles, looking for a meal.

Thick, burgundy carpets and cushions with complex, flowery designs lay spread out under the greenery, forming some kind of meeting place, and Ben sank onto them, feeling empty inside. He watched Hakim prepare cardamom tea over a fire-pit, then hand him a steaming cup. Ben drank slowly while watching Hakim go about his cleaning tasks in his usual calm manner until drowsiness pulled him into a deep sleep.

By the time he woke, dusk had fallen. Several people had gathered in a circle on the carpets. They sat cross-legged on the cushions, chatting and sharing food from large trays placed in the middle. Ben's appetite awakened to the smells of grilled fish and lamb, yellow rice with chickpeas and dates, and other delicacies that he could not name. He snuck some pieces of meat under his tunic to give to the falcon later, then watched as people bustled about, lighting fires, serving more cardamom tea, and chuckling at each other's stories. A couple of camels settled under the palm trees.

Someone picked up a chalice drum and began beating on it in a repetitive manner, though not loudly enough to drown out the conversation. After a while, another drum joined in, then a third. Slowly, the rhythmic music silenced the chatting, the food and refreshing night ignited people's energy, and the flickering fires and relative gloom invited some to dance.

Ben watched as men stepped back and forth and to the side, holding a thin stick that they waved around them as they moved to the rhythm of the well-practiced beats. He became completely absorbed by this tiny concentration of life in the desert until someone suddenly dropped a drum in his hands. He stared at it shyly, then tapped on it with the tips of his fingers, afraid to break the cadence with his inexperience. The pulse was captivating, though, and echoed the sound of his heart, releasing his pain, and Ben found himself thumping harder and harder as the frenzy of the music took over the participants. Each became lost in their bubble, entranced, yet also connected by the single thread of primeval life that emanated from the drums.

By the time they were done, Ben's muscles hurt, and he breathed heavily, his eyes stinging. He leaned with his forehead against the drum until he could control himself again.

When he lifted his head, Hakim had left the circle.

Ben sprang to his feet, searching the darkness. Stepping away from the oasis, he stretched out his arm absentmindedly, sensing the falcon nearby. The bird landed on his arm, asking for its treat.

"Hakim, wait!" Ben called, spotting the trainer heading towards the property. Ben ran after him, panting from carrying the heavy falcon. "Hakim, you're the only one I can talk to. I... I can't stay here. You see, there are things I need to do, urgent things. It's a long story, but I need your help."

Hakim stared at the bird as it nibbled on the piece of meat Ben had given it. "Falcon is national emblem of my country," he said, petting the bird gently. "The bond between falcon and my people is as old as time. Bird bring pride and honour to he who owns it." He paused. "This is wild falcon, yet it come to you willingly..." He turned and walked on, his head slightly cocked as if in deep thought.

Something startled the falcon, and it flew off, making both Hakim and Ben look up at the same time.

The Sheikh's son stood on a terrace, staring down at them. Zayed stayed long enough to make sure they knew he had seen them, then disappeared into his room.

"Sad story," Hakim said in broken English, startling Ben. "Do you know why Sadalbari so important?"

Ben shook his head.

"Zayed's mother, great horse whisperer. Teach son to ride. Mother and son share same passion. One day, she hear of legendary horse lost in dunes. How wild horse survive is a mystery. She go search with Zayed and some men. They discover great horse." Hakim bowed his head. "But her kind heart not touch Sadalbari and Sadalbari kill her under hoof."

Ben's eyes bulged.

"Very sad," Hakim repeated. "Heart of Sheikh Azhar broken. Zayed precious son to him. Only thing left. But father and son fight, always, no love left, until a month ago when Sheikh Azhar find and capture Sadalbari. Horse was still alive. A miracle! He hope to please son, he hope son ride horse that kill his mother, like a victory, but son never happy." He glanced at Ben with fiery eyes and said in a clear voice, "You try to tame Sadalbari, but perhaps is Sheikh's son that need attention." He let the sentence hang before giving a short bow and disappearing into the night.

Ben stared after him, stunned. He had asked Hakim for help, and the horse trainer had given him an answer. Hakim was telling him that perhaps it wasn't the horse he needed to befriend; perhaps it was Zayed.

CHAPTER 15 *Wild Goose Chase*

The spaceship skimmed across a lake and slid through the folds of snow-covered mountains. Mesmo landed the craft in the shadow of Reinebringen, a sharp-edged mountain overlooking a tiny Norwegian village on the Lofoten Islands.

This was where he had previously met Einar when he had come to recover the Wise One's Toreq key. There had been no enmity between them, then. Einar had even displayed sadness on hearing of Mesmo's daughter passing. Einar had given him the key, proud to be handing over his life's work and to have been of service to the Toreq, as had been done in his family for countless generations.

It had been a solemn, respectful ceremony. No more.

But that had been before Mesmo decided to live on Earth permanently. And before he had asked the Wise Ones to stop being silent witnesses to humans ravaging the Earth and become active teachers instead.

That had not gone down well with Einar.

The Norseman had accused him of turning against his own people and disrespecting the Toreq Arch Council who had sent him to Earth in the first place. He had called for a vote among the seven Wise Ones to strip Mesmo of his Toreq citizenship, thereby rendering his authority over the Wise Ones meaningless.

Mesmo thought about this as he hiked to Einar's home village. Had he really turned his back on the Arch Council? He didn't think so.

The Arch Council did not randomly send an Observer to Earth. He had gone through a thorough and meticulous selection process. There had been many applicants. And they had chosen *him*.

It meant he had been given the Council's full support. It also meant that, whatever his decision about whether humans should be allowed to continue to live or not, the Council would have listened and accepted his position. Only, he had not been able to go back to the Mother Planet to give the Arch Council his full report.

Not that it had really mattered. The simple fact that he had chosen not to return to Torequ'ai but live on Earth instead, had sent a strong signal that there was still something on Earth worth fighting for. Humans should not yet be blasted out of existence.

It had never been a question of choosing sides. Living among humans did not mean he had turned his back on his people. It had meant he was sending a powerful statement to tell his people to *wait!* Give humans another chance.

By now, Mesmo had reached the outskirts of Einar's land: a wide patch of grass topped by a red-coloured house with white window-frames that overlooked majestic fjords and mountains. To the right of the house stood a lower building with a couple of small windows. It was like any other home in the quaint village, offering Einar a quiet, low-key cover from where he could fulfil his research on human activity. Just like Akeya's home had been, or any of the other Wise Ones, for that matter.

Mesmo observed the dwelling from afar, glad that the frosty evening did not affect him as it would humans. A single light shone on the side of the lower building.

He waited. Could Einar be hiding here, in plain sight?

Darkness fell, and still, nothing moved. His phone buzzed in his jacket pocket. It was a message from Amaru: ALL ACCOUNTED FOR. EXCEPT EINAR. LOCATION UNKNOWN.

Mesmo stared from the phone to the house. 'All accounted for'. The remaining four Wise Ones were safe and in hiding. Amaru had made sure of this once Mesmo had told him of Akeya's death. That left Einar. Could the Norseman really have committed the heinous deed of killing two of the Wise Ones?

And what could that mean for Ben? Had Einar kidnapped him? And if so, for what reason?

Gritting his teeth, Mesmo left his hiding spot and jogged to Einar's house. He glanced through the windows, rushing from one to the other, before trying the front door. It was unlocked.

He didn't feel like being careful anymore. Time was ticking. He needed to find Ben.

"Einar!" he called through the dark home. It was time for a face-to-face confrontation.

When only silence answered, Mesmo rushed through the rooms, searching downstairs and up.

There was no sign of Einar.

Then he was outside again, heading for the other building, which had its light on. This time the door was locked.

Mesmo looked through the small window, but it was too dark inside to see anything. He slammed against it, calling Einar's name, until the door gave way and he was inside.

It was Einar's research and workspace. There was a big table strewn with documents in the middle. The walls were full of maps and photographs.

Mesmo studied the pictures that Einar had taken of various volcanoes, remembering that, in the human world, Einar was a volcanologist. It gave him a reason to travel without calling for attention.

Mesmo crashed into the next room, which was strewn with old furniture covered in dust.

"Einar!" he yelled again, balling his fists.

Where *was* he?

Mesmo went back to the workroom, kicked at a chair and shoved papers off the table. They fluttered to the ground around him. He leaned on the table, his eyes falling on a single map taped to it. It was a map of Europe. Five red circles indicated volcanoes around the continent.

Why did he feel like he was playing a game of cat and mouse? Where was Ben? Where was Einar? Why had Su Tai and Akeya been killed? He just couldn't put the pieces together.

Breathing hard, Mesmo stared at the heavily circled spots. Though it felt like Einar was sending him on a wild goose chase, Mesmo knew he would have to check out each of these circled locations.

Mesmo tore the map from the table and headed outside. He was met with a starlit night. He stared at the sky, then picked up his phone and dialled Laura's number.

"Mesmo?" she said, sounding tired but hopeful.

Mesmo breathed in. "No news yet," he said. "I just wanted to see how you're holding up."

"I'll be fine once Ben is home," she said. He heard her suck on her inhaler. They fell silent for a moment.

"Are you coming back?" she asked finally.

Mesmo closed his eyes. "No. Not until I find Ben."

Her voice sounded distant. "I don't know what I'd do without you," she said.

Mesmo considered her words. "Without me," he said. "You wouldn't be in this mess."

CHAPTER 16 *Missed Opportunity*

The stairs on the outside of Zayed's apartments did not have a railing. They followed the wall and were cut out of the beige adobe.

Ben reached the terrace bordering the apartment, and found one of the doors open. Inside, a couple of screens stood on a white shelf against the wall of a small living-room. In front of them, Zayed sat, propped on a white leather sofa, fingers moving rapidly over a gaming control.

The light from inside dimmed suddenly, and Zayed's bodyguard filled the doorway.

Ben caught his breath, but Zayed barked an order, and the bodyguard left. Ben bit his tongue to pick up courage. He entered the room, which he found strewn with expensive and odd-looking toys such as a drone, a stereo set, a mariachi hat, a finely carved Spanish guitar, and piles of books.

A high volume of cold air from an air conditioning sped through Ben's hair, then fled through the open door and windows into the night.

Zayed did not look up from his game. He stuck his tongue in his cheek and grunted as his avatar battled evil monsters in a gold mine.

Ben watched him play for a while, acutely aware that Zayed was connected to the internet. And to make matters worse, Zayed's shiny smartphone lay on the sofa beside him. Ben stared at it, feeling drawn to it like a magnet.

Swallowing through his dry throat, Ben tried to look casual and spotted a second gaming control. Without saying a word, he picked it up and began playing alongside Zayed's avatar. They battled the monsters for a while, almost getting knocked over several times, but Ben protected Zayed's avatar until they reached a mighty portal.

LEVEL 10 COMPLETE, the screen flashed at them.

"There's a treasure behind that portal," Ben said.

Zayed pressed play. "You're pretty good," he said, narrowly avoiding a fiery dragon.

"Thanks," Ben said. "I play with Mesm... m-my dad." He barely got through the sentence.

Having lost interest, Ben dropped the gaming console and strolled around the room instead. He was curious to find out more about Zayed, but also found himself constantly glancing back at the phone. Zayed was so focused on the game, would he notice if Ben fished it off the sofa?

Fighting the urge to do so, Ben lingered in front of a well-stocked bookshelf instead. He needed to think, not act rashly.

How can I get Zayed away from the phone?

He must have stood there too long because Zayed said, "You can pick one if you want."

Ben jumped. It was as if the guy had eyes on the back of his head. Blinking, Ben focused on the books even though reading was the last thing on his mind. "Thanks," he said, staring at the titles for the first time. He recognized many famous authors: William Shakespeare, Victor Hugo, Ernest Hemingway, Paulo Coelho... Most books were in their original language.

He glanced at Zayed, fascinated by the idea that the teen had mastered all these languages well enough to read these classics.

Ben pulled out a book that he had read at school and which happened to be in English: *The*

Little Prince by French author Antoine de Saint-Exupéry. Even as he flipped through the pages, he kept an eye on Zayed's phone until he got distracted by underlined passages and hand-written notes in the book. His finger slid down the page and paused. *"You become responsible forever for what you have tamed[5],"* he read. He lifted his head from the book and glanced nervously at Zayed.

Had the teen heard him?

Yes. Zayed's avatar was getting hammered by a troll, yet his fingers did nothing on the gaming control to defend it. Ben wasn't sure he knew why he had read that particular quote. Maybe he wanted to make sure Zayed understood he'd be responsible for Sadalbari forever if the horse were ever tamed.

Zayed's cold voice startled him. *"To me, you are still nothing more than a little boy who is just like a hundred thousand other little boys. And I have no need of you. And you, on your part, have no need of me.[6]"*

---

[5] *The Little Prince* by French author Antoine de Saint-Exupéry

[6] *The Little Prince* by French author Antoine de Saint-Exupéry

Ben gulped. Zayed had quoted *The Little Prince* from memory.

Ben knew it wasn't the full quote. There was more to it. Something about friendship... But the fact Zayed stopped there and returned to his game told him enough. Hand shaking, Ben returned the book to its shelf and pretended to be unaffected by Zayed's choice of words.

He strolled around and stared at a simple painting hanging next to the bookshelf. Only dark beige had been used, and the few brush lines that had been made came from a firm hand that mastered thick and light strokes. Within the handful of twirling streaks, Ben discovered the abstract form of a horse, which he easily recognized as Sadalbari. And next to Sadalbari, yet further in the distance among the dunes, a beautiful woman in a tunic looked into the distance, her face veiled except for her eyes.

The work was simple yet powerful and clearly executed by an experienced artist.

"That's beautiful," Ben said as lightly as possible, bending closer to see if he could make out the curly Arabic writing at the bottom. "What does it say here?" he asked.

Zayed grunted as he clicked with his fingers on the gaming control. "It says, *Star Rider.*"

Goosebumps rose on Ben's arms. *Star Rider!* How fitting. And how tragic. So, if this was Zayed's mother in the background, why was she not riding the horse, as indicated in the painting's name?

"I wonder who made this?" he said half to himself.

Zayed's eyes were glued to the game. "I did."

Ben pulled back and gawked at the teenager, wondering if he had heard him right, but Zayed didn't acknowledge him. It wasn't long before Ben discovered more of Zayed's artwork: canvases, piled together in a corner.

He studied them, one after the other, astounded by their uncluttered and natural beauty. They all represented Arabian purebreds in the desert.

"I don't know much about art," Ben admitted, "but these are amazing! You should get them into art galleries and stuff."

Zayed snorted. "As if that'll ever happen."

"Why not?" Ben stated. *Didn't this guy always get what he wanted?*

"My father is a billionaire. He extracts oil from the ground and sells it to the world. I'm his only child and heir. Do the math."

Ben thought about that. "You must be lonely out here," he said.

Zayed didn't answer, so Ben added, "What about school?"

Zayed humphed. "School? I have never set foot in a school. I have had the best tutors from England, France, the United States, and the Arab world. I have been groomed to take over my father's company and follow in his footsteps."

"Haven't you tried talking to him?" Ben ventured, but instantly knew he had gone a step too far because Zayed's posture tensed.

"Do you not have anything better to do, whisperer?"

Ben instinctively knew he had lost Zayed's patience, so he went back to the first painting and said, "I'm sorry about your mother."

Zayed's fingers froze over the controls, and his avatar fell into a chasm. His voice was bitter. "I know what you're trying to do, whisperer. It is Sadalbari you are here for, not me."

"I'm just trying to understand the rider, so I can better deal with the horse."

Zayed set his jaw. "Then you are wasting your time. And you are wasting mine. Get out!"

That was it. That was as far as Ben was going to get.

This time....

Ben was going to step out when the

bodyguard appeared in the doorway with an urgent look on his face. He spoke rapidly, and his words made Zayed jump from his sofa.

"What is it?" Ben asked fearfully.

"Something's wrong with the horses! Let's go!" Zayed shouted, sprinting into action and disappearing after the bodyguard.

Ben's heart rate quickened. He was alone in Zayed's quarters. The computers were right there. The smartphone still on the sofa. A quick email. A call for help. It wouldn't take long…

But Nutmeg was in trouble.

The internet will have to wait.

He leapt out of the room, dashed through the door, and slammed into Zayed. The teen had been waiting for him on the other side.

"Ouch!" Ben yelled in surprise, rubbing his nose.

The bodyguard grabbed his arm.

"Do you think I'm that stupid?" Zayed seethed. "I saw you look at my phone the minute you came in." Zayed took Ben's wrist and held it up between them. "Did you really think I believed you came here to *make friends*?" He looked at Ben's hand, only to find it empty. Scowling, he slipped back into his room and returned with his smartphone. "You're stretching my patience, whisperer. Mark my words: you *will* get me on that horse!" He shot Ben an angry glance. "Let's go," he said before heading off.

The bodyguard pulled Ben along, having to support him several times because his legs were like jelly from shock. His hopes of ever using the phone or the internet in shambles. But as they neared the stables, Ben's dismay was replaced by a rushing in his ears and a tingling in his hands. The alien skill awoke within him.

Several men had gathered at the arena, holding torches in the air. They yelled at each other, arguing who would enter the stables.

Ben could hear Nutmeg's cry of fear long before he reached the stables. He overtook Zayed and pushed his way through the crowd to enter the gloomy stables.

Nutmeg! What's wrong?

He rushed to the horse's stall. A group of men stood watching while one man waved a torch inside the stable.

Snake, Benjamin! There's a snake!

A snake? Relief washed over Ben. Okay, he could handle a snake. *Don't be afraid. I'll get it out.*

He grabbed the torch off another man and entered Nutmeg's stall.

The horse huffed, ears laid back and coat

glistening with sweat. The other horses stamped their hooves, terrified.

Ben held up his hand at them. *Stay still, now.*

The horses calmed down at once, something which did not go unnoticed by the men.

Ben searched the stall for a sign of the snake, but the torch caused shadows to appear, making it hard to discern anything. He needed to listen with his mind, not look with his eyes. He crouched down in the middle of the stall and let the skill run its course.

Something slithered and coiled at the edge of his mind, along with a sense of intense fear. Ben lifted the torch to illuminate the left corner of the stall, and that's when he heard a sizzling sound.

The man behind him jumped back, shouting, "Alharia! Alharia!" Startled by the man's cries, Ben stepped back, bumping into Zayed, who had also entered the stall.

"Alharia," the teen hissed behind him. "Deadly snake. One bite, and you are as good as gone, whisperer."

Ben set his jaw. He handed Zayed his torch, relying only on his skill to scan the gloomy stall. He crouched down and concentrated on the snake.

I am Benjamin Archer. May I speak with

you?

The snake hissed but seemed somewhat relieved to make contact.

I am Echiss. Sstay at disstance or I sstrike!

I will stay at a distance, I promise, but you are causing a lot of panic by staying here.

Me? Caussing panic? There iss sstomping hoovess, burning fire, sshouting men. It iss I who panic the mosst.

I understand. I can help you get out of here. Let me set you free.

Outsside iss falcon, chasing me. I sstay and hide.

I see... Then I will have a word with the falcon, too.

Echis coiled into C-shapes, rubbing its scales together to make a sizzling sound like water on a hot pan.

Nutmeg flinched.

Ben was short on patience. He snapped at the snake. *Will you stop that? If you stay, you'll get trampled—unless these men kill you first. You need to trust me.*

Echis thought for a moment, its marble eyes gleaming at Ben. *Alright. But sstop sstaring at me. It makess me edgy. I bitess when I edgy.*

Ben looked away quickly. *Okay, okay. I'm*

sorry. He stretched out his arm.

Echis hesitated, then slithered towards him, slipped up his forearm and remained there like a wristband. The snake was smaller and lighter than Ben had expected. It had crimson spots with black rings on its white skin, and a round snout on its head. Ben tried to avoid looking at its eyes.

Are you ready?

Echis hissed uneasily with its forked tongue, so Ben added, *It'll be okay, I promise.*

He stood slowly and faced the circle of wide-eyed men who hunkered back as soon as he stepped towards them. As he left the stall and then the stable, Echis coiled into his hands and scanned the skies fearfully.

Just as Ben looked up, the falcon descended from the night sky, claws outstretched.

Ben yelled, *Hey! You can't have this one!*

He stooped over Echis just as the falcon swooped over him, then headed up to the skies again to gather speed. Ben ran towards the dunes, but the falcon attacked again and made him drop the snake this time. Ben threw himself over the snake to protect it, yelling, *I said, you can't have this one!*

The falcon rose and circled at a distance, then came back and landed heavily on Ben's arm.

Calm down for a minute, will you? I promised to keep this snake safe. I'm sorry, falcon, but you'll have to get your dinner elsewhere.

The falcon flapped its wings haughtily and took to the skies again. Ben watched it disappear into the night. A rush of calm washed over the snake.

Thhank you, Benjamin Archer.

They reached the dunes, and Echis shoved its body into the sand until only its eyes stuck out—the perfect camouflage.

Ben nodded, relieved at the outcome. *Watch yourself now. And don't go back to the stables. I might not be there to save you next time.*

Echis hissed in agreement.

Ben turned.

The Sheikh's son stood not far away, fists clenched. "I see the media were right about you, after all," Zayed said with an icy tone that made Ben's blood go cold. The teen turned and strode away, shouting over his shoulder, "Get some sleep, whisperer. I expect to ride Sadalbari by morning."

CHAPTER 17 *Submission*

When Zayed appeared at the arena the next morning, he looked fresh and well-rested.

Ben, on the other hand, hadn't slept a wink. He had tossed and turned, unable to sleep. His mind had become obsessed with his missed opportunity to use Zayed's computers or smartphone. Caught up in nightmares, he had watched himself sneak into Zayed's room, type a quick email, then hover his finger over the send button...

Over and over, the feverish dream had repeated itself, to the point where it had woken Ben and kept him pacing his room until morning. A hundred ways to use the computers to reach help had crossed his mind, but every time the bodyguards cast a shadow over his plans. When the sun rose, Ben had had to give up on his grand plans for escape.

Now, standing inside the arena, he glared at Zayed, because that was all he had left of his pride. He didn't have a shred of a plan for what to do and felt certain the teen wouldn't care if he ended up trampled by the white stallion.

Sadalbari neighed from within the stables, anxious to vent its anger on something—or someone—after being cooped up for days.

Only half a dozen people had come this time.

Zayed clicked his fingers, indicating the horse should be brought forth.

Ben braced himself.

"Zayed!" A voice boomed from the top of the stairs. The teenager's head snapped around. Sheikh Azhar stood at the top of the stairs, looking down at him. Zayed opened his mouth to say something, but his dad turned and walked away. Zayed shot a hateful glance Ben's way, then stood and joined his father. Both disappeared into the property. And just like that, the show was cancelled.

Ben let his arms drop to his sides. Muscles slacking, he followed the Sheikh and his son from a distance, realizing only now how tense he had been.

Father and son quarrelled all the way to Zayed's apartments.

Listening to the tone of voices rising, Ben could easily imagine that this type of arguing was a regular event at the Sheikh's property. It reminded him of the heated debate he'd heard on his arrival. Only, he hadn't known then who the voices had belonged to back then.

Unable to act on anything, Ben turned and headed back to the stables. The purebreds now greeted him with respect for having removed the snake from their midst.

Nutmeg's head popped over the stall. *What are you doing, Benjamin?*

Ben didn't reply. He continued to the end of the stable, where Sadalbari was being held behind high wooden doors.

Nutmeg neighed worriedly.

Ben opened one of the doors and slipped inside. Sadalbari's pure-white body glowed in the dusty gloom. The door slid closed behind Ben, and as his eyes grew accustomed to the darkness, he watched the powerful stallion.

Sadalbari stood unmoving, a long chain, attached from its neck to the wall, holding it in place.

"You're stuck here, too, aren't you?" Ben breathed.

Without warning, Sadalbari lunged.

Ben yelled, falling back in shock. The chain tensed, pulling back the horse. It snorted in anger. *Leave, Fly, or you'll regret it!*

Ben stood, his own anger welling. *Just stop that! You sound like Zayed.*

Sadalbari reared in fury. *How dare you!*

Ben stood his ground. The chain tensed and held. The stallion calmed down. Horse and boy glared at each other.

Ben sank into a crouching position as his anger ebbed away. He studied the horse, suddenly moved by sadness. *You don't belong here.*

It was true. This mighty steed belonged with the desert, wild and untamed.

I can set you free.

Sadalbari pawed at the ground. *And why would you do that, Fly?*

Ben watched him closely. *Because I can.*

Sadalbari considered him. *You lie. It is a trick.*

It's not a trick! You don't belong here. You belong out there, roaming the desert, the way you always have.

Sadalbari did not disagree with him, so Ben stood slowly and stepped towards the end of the chain.

Sadalbari followed him closely, challenging him. *You would not do such a thing.*

Ben reached for the pin in the wall but his hand froze. *I would, but you have to promise me that you will not harm the Sheikh's son.*

The stallion snorted, and Ben's stomach clenched.

Sadalbari, I can set you free, but you have to promise me you won't hurt Zayed.

Do it, then, Fly. Set me free. What are you waiting for?

Ben's hand trembled over the pin, because Sadalbari had not validated his request. He saw it with his mind. The second he released the chain, Sadalbari would crash through the doors, gallop to find Zayed, and then he would... he would... Ben caught his breath.

The stallion snorted in irritation. *Release me! DO IT!*

But Ben knew that he couldn't. And Sadalbari knew that he knew.

With a split second to save himself, Ben dropped to the ground, narrowly avoiding the stomping hooves. He rolled to the door, slamming into it, just as Sadalbari lurched towards him. The chain tensed, snapping him back. Sadalbari blared in rage.

Ben watched, panting, as the horse shook its mane in a maddening craze. *You would rather cause harm than recover your freedom!*

Sadalbari snorted. *The King of the Desert will not be disgraced into becoming a mere horse for mounting. Zayed will pay for this insult. And when I am done with him, I will come for you!*

Ben staggered back on his hands and feet, finding the opening in the door through which he had come. He rolled out, the door shutting behind him. He stood and teetered toward Nutmeg's stall, trembling.

Nutmeg peered at him over the fence. *Benjamin, are you all right?*

Ben grabbed the edge of the stall and kicked it hard.

Nutmeg snorted.

Ben kicked again, venting his frustration, then leaned into Nutmeg's head and wrapped his arms around the horse's neck.

Nutmeg nuzzled him. *You are sad.*

Ben stopped petting her.

She nudged him. *Come. Lie with me.*

Letting himself be led, Ben entered the stall.

Nutmeg lowered to the ground and tucked her legs under her body, so Ben could sit and lean into her.

Nutmeg nibbled his neck. *Tell me, again, about the green hills.*

Ben sighed and brought forth images of home, perched on the hill overlooking the valley of Chilliwack, with its mountain range in the distance, the green cornfields, the fresh grass. He imagined himself lying under the maple tree, watching the sun shimmer through the leaves, and Mesmo sitting nearby, telling him about distant planets.

He fell asleep, holding on to that image.

* * *

A scream pierced the air.

Ben jolted up. "What was that?" he yelled, hurriedly blinking the sleep from his eyes. The night caught him off guard.

Nutmeg scrambled to her feet.

Boy and horse scanned the darkness, fully alert.

BANG!

The doors to Sadalbari's stall flew open. The stallion emerged like a bullet, dashing before them in a flurry of white, the chain dangling from its neck. Another scream escaped its muzzle—not from pain or fear, but searing fury. Ben almost missed the fact that someone had jumped from a fence onto the stallion's back.

"Oh, no! Zayed!" he yelled, overcome with horror. "He's going to get killed!"

Nutmeg neighed, already in position by the stall's fence.

Ben clambered on her back. "Hurry, Nutmeg!"

Nutmeg dashed out of the stables into the starlit night; Ben clamped on her back.

Shouts of alarm came from the adobe houses, torches were lit, footsteps thudded on the stairs. Nutmeg did not wait for help to come, but galloped across the flat area leading to the oasis, then on to the desert.

Ben held on so tight he thought he'd tear Nutmeg's hair out of her mane. He peeked through his closed eyelids and found Sadalbari clambering over the first dune, Zayed still hanging on by using the chain around the horse's neck.

We've got to catch up! Can you do it?

Nutmeg snorted. *I am not native to this land, but I will do my best. Hang on!*

Ben hung on.

Nutmeg reached the first dune and struggled to the top. Ben caught his breath. The full moon laid a mantle of soft light on the endless waves of dunes, briefly reminding him of a distant ocean...

I see them!

Nutmeg's words snapped Ben out of the memory. He caught sight of Sadalbari, as the stallion slipped behind a dune some ways ahead.

Quick, Nutmeg!

The Sheik's estate disappeared behind them as if swallowed by the earth. Muffled silence closed in on them as Nutmeg struggled up and down the mounds of sand. They barely reached the place where they had last seen Sadalbari when the white stallion emerged and careened into them.

Nutmeg lost her footing, sending both she and Ben flying down a dune.

"Nutmeg!" Ben cried, picking himself up. He coughed up sand and rushed to his friend. *Are you okay?*

Nutmeg breathed heavily. *Am ok-kay. S-save yourself.*

Above them, at the top of the dune, Sadalbari reared, back hooves thrust high in the air, and Zayed somersaulted off the stallion with a yell. The teenager's body landed with a thud in the sand.

Ben scrambled up the treacherous dune, slipping and losing his footing several times. But when he reached the top, Sadalbari was waiting for him.

The stallion glowed in the moonlight like a vengeful ghost, the chain that hung from its neck clanging. It snorted and nudged a hoof at Zayed's terrified form, like a lion toying with its upcoming meal. It glanced Ben's way, making sure Ben was watching, then leapt on its hind legs, aiming to strike.

"NOOO!" Ben flung his hands towards the stallion, the alien skill gushing through his arms, unstoppable, more powerful than ever before. It exploded from every blood cell, outward and upward, reaching the sky in a scarlet glare, lashing at Sadalbari like a whip.

Sadalbari screeched, hit full-on by the force of the skill. It struggled against Ben's will as the boy forced the stallion to its knees.

Ben gasped, terrified by his own strength, feeling the skill bend the horse's will to his own—like a dam that had burst, releasing uncontrollable power. He staggered towards the stallion; his mind the horse's mind, his limbs the horse's limbs, his will crushing the horse's will.

Sadalbari was no match. The stallion slumped to the side, whimpering, the whites of its eyes protruding in fear. Its flank rose in short bursts, as though a giant were sitting on it.

Ben dropped to his knees. He plunged his fists into the sand, shutting his eyes tight, desperate to shut the floodgates on this unlimited and irresistible power. He was an inch from losing total control. He persisted. The skill obeyed— barely. It simmered and deflated, seeping back into Ben's body, docile and submissive.

Ben gasped, gathering his senses, still hunched down on all fours. Then, he lifted his head and looked at Sadalbari. The stallion lay on its side, breathing heavily. The King of the Desert had fallen.

Overcome with crushing guilt, Ben crawled forward and bent his forehead on to the stallion's muzzle. *I'm sorry! I'm so sorry!* He sobbed. The skill vibrated in his core as he tried to soothe the stallion with the same mind that had just defeated it.

Hurried footsteps surrounded him, torches flared through his closed eyelids, and men commented in awe.

Afterwards, Ben would think what a strange sight it must have been to see the mighty steed at his mercy, lying, terrified, in the middle of an ocean of dunes.

But right then, this new level of power floored him, and he understood, now, why the Toreq forbade the use of the skill to bend another to their will. The skill fed on the opportunity like a starving dragon, almost taking a life of its own. Had it not been for sheer willpower, Ben would have lost control of it, turning the mighty stallion into a helpless puppet. The thought rattled him.

Sounds around him told him that Zayed and Nutmeg were being led away, surrounded by people who had come to their aid from the oasis. Hands pulled him away from Sadalbari.

I'm sorry! The words repeated in his mind over and over. He hadn't meant to do it. He hadn't meant to hurt Sadalbari. Or break him. It had never been his intention. *I didn't know. I'm so sorry.*

Why hadn't Mesmo warned him? Why hadn't he told Ben what the skill was capable of?

Sadalbari huffed as it obediently followed the men that took it away. Only Ben remained, eyes still shut, crouching with his hands over his head, his forehead touching the sand.

"Sabi," Abdul said, touching his arm. "Boy, come." He rolled Ben over and grunted as he lifted him in his arms.

Utterly numb, feeling disconnected from his body, Ben watched the moon lower on the horizon as Abdul carried him back to the estate.

CHAPTER 18 *Absolution*

Night turned to morning, and still Ben remained by the arena. Abdul had tried to convince him to rest in his room, but Ben wouldn't budge. He'd sat on a bench, stuffed his fingers through his disheveled hair and stared at the ground for hours. Abdul had placed a blanket over his shoulders, then left him alone, for which he was grateful.

When the first ray of sharp sunlight landed on the stables, a man—who was not Hakim—brought forth Sadalbari. The horse followed obediently, twitching and flapping its ears, as if bothered by a fly.

Feeling nauseated, Ben leaned back on the bench and spied on the stallion between spaces in the fence. Sadalbari had lost its sheen, its neck no longer stood erect with pride but hung as if in shame. Ben pulled in his legs, tears streaming down his face. He had done this. He had broken Sadalbari, just like Zayed had wanted him to.

As if on cue, the Sheik's son appeared and stood by the fence. He rested his chin on his arms without noticing Ben and stared at the stallion. Ben tried to contain his feelings. He didn't want Zayed to see him crying, so he swiftly wiped his eyes with the back of his sleeve.

The horse trainer turned to Zayed and waved him over, inviting the Sheihk's son to mount the stallion. Zayed shook his head.

Ben went rigid. *What?* He stared at Zayed, utterly shocked. Emotions boiled and bubbled from the pit of his stomach all the way up to his burning cheeks. Something snapped within him. Without thinking, he leapt to his feet and lunged at the teen. He slammed into Zayed, sending both of them hurtling to the ground.

"Tired of your new toy already?" Ben yelled, overcome with fury. He knew he was no match for Zayed, who was a head taller than him, but he didn't care. He swung his fists clumsily at the struggling teen, both of them sending sand up around them.

Ben expected to get a good beating, but, instead, to his surprise, Zayed didn't fight back. The teen raised his arms in defence without saying anything. Ben stared at Zayed. He wanted to hit the teen so badly, but Zayed's lack of response diffused his anger. He contained himself and sat there, panting, then dropped on his back beside Zayed because he knew, deep down, that it wasn't really the teen that had made him angry. It was himself. They stayed like that, breathing heavily, covered in sand. A long moment passed before either of them spoke.

"Do you know how many 'toys' my father gave me this year?" Zayed asked, his voice devoid of accusation toward Ben's attack.

Ben scrunched up his face. He hadn't expected Zayed to actually answer his question. Was the guy really going to brag about his fortune right now? "How should I know?" he snapped.

"Around forty," Zayed answered, unaffected by Ben's vehemence. "Top-notch, ultra-luxurious toys: cars, horses, the finest shoes, the most expensive watches. And do you know," he added, "how many times I've seen my father this year?"

Ben frowned, turning his head to look at the teen.

"Five times," Zayed said. "Three at the

beginning of the year and twice since you've been here. The five times he has come to see me were because I misbehaved." He sighed. "Only then, it seems, am I worthy of a visit."

Ben stared at the teen. Was Zayed playing games with him? The teen's eyes were empty and sad, not cold and arrogant like before, as if he was showing Ben his true self for the first time. No. Zayed wasn't toying with him.

Ben looked at the sky, imagining what it would have been like to only see his mother five times a year. He had grown up without a dad. Zayed had grown up without a mother. In that respect, they weren't that much different. Ben could fully understand the sense of loss that came with the absence of a parent.

Without a dad at home, Ben had spent a lot of time on his own because his mother had had to work long hours to make ends meet. But he'd seen her every day, even if it had sometimes only been for a few minutes because she was exhausted.

But five times?

"Why only five times?" he asked.

Zayed shrugged, blinking at the sky. "I guess I stopped existing when my mother died. My father buried himself in his work. He sends me gifts, the best tutors; he throws me big parties, as if he thinks these things will fill the void between us. When he found Sadalbari, he thought dominating the stallion that killed my mother would make me happy." He paused. "*I* thought it would make me happy." He turned away, his voice muffled. "But it hasn't. Nothing will bring her back."

Zayed had Ben's full attention now. He frowned and stared at the teen. "Zayed, what was it that happened the first time you tried to ride Sadalbari?"

Zayed lifted his arm to his face and Ben realized he was crying. It took the teen a while to find his voice. "My mother took me into the desert," Zayed said. "There were rumors that a mighty stallion had been found. My mother wanted to show me how she could mount a wild horse without breaking it. She was really good at that, you know?"

He sniffed, then continued, "We found Sadalbari near an oasis. My mother approached it, the way she always would a wild animal, with gentle, respectful movements. It was like she was dancing." He paused to remember. "And then, she got on Sadalbari's back. It took her all week to do that. I had gotten bored. I wanted some action..."

Ben held his breath.

Zayed swallowed. "She... she felt it was safe

for me to mount Sadalbari with her. We'd been around many horses together before. I wasn't afraid. But I was impatient. I wanted to see Sadalbari gallop. I wanted to see what this mighty stallion was capable of. And I... I..." he broke off.

"What?"

"I... I smacked Sadalbari. I was only a child. I always did that when I mounted horses at home, to get them galloping. It was a habit. But Sadalbari went berserk." Zayed looked away, his voice sad and distant. "I don't remember much after that."

Ben stared at the teen, a shiver going up and down his spine. He could imagine what happened after that. He shut his eyes in the hopes of stopping the images.

Zayed's muffled voice reached him. "I was only six," he said.

"Does your father know about this?"

Zayed shook his head, still looking away.

"I think you should tell him," Ben said softly.

Zayed faced him. "Why do you think I do the things that I do? They are the only way I can get my father's attention. I always hope he'll stay long enough for me to tell him. But we only end up fighting instead."

Ben sat up. "You can't keep this inside, Zayed. It was a terrible accident. You couldn't have predicted the outcome." His heart constricted, remembering what he had just done with the skill. Had that been an accident, too?

Zayed sighed. He stood slowly and stared at Sadalbari, then at Ben, his face downcast. "Pack your bags, whisperer. It's time you went home," he said, then turned to go.

It took Ben a fraction of a second to realize what Zayed's words meant. He blinked and jumped up. "Wait! What about Sadalbari?"

Zayed stopped without turning around. "What about him?"

"You have to tell him!"

Zayed looked at Ben, one eyebrow lifted.

"I'm serious!" Ben said, standing steadfast. He took Zayed by the arm and led him to the fence. He nodded at the stallion. "Tell him. Everything! Tell him you didn't mean to do what you did, that it was an accident."

Zayed stared at Ben as if he were crazy but said nothing. He pressed his lips together and considered the horse. "Will you come with me?" he asked, neither pleading nor ordering. It was more like an invitation.

Ben shook his head vehemently, a lump forming in his throat. "I... I can't... You have to do it on your own." How could he explain that the proximity of the skill terrorized the stallion?

Zayed bit his lip. *"You become responsible forever for what you've tamed*[7], isn't that right, whisperer?" he said, glancing at Ben.

They stared at each other. Then, Ben nodded.

Zayed puffed his cheeks and entered the arena. He advanced towards the stallion, speaking in a hushed tone. Sadalbari shifted and twitched on its hooves. The horse's ears flickered back and forth, its eyes following the teen, until they were facing each other.

Zayed spoke to it in a low voice for a long time, hands outstretched. He did not move, giving the horse some space.

Ben watched in awe, as horse and boy considered each other; assessed each other's sincerity.

Then, after countless minutes that could have been hours, Sadalbari stooped forward and placed its muzzle in Zayed's hands.

Zayed shot a glance Ben's way. It was full of wonder.

Ben let out a long breath, realizing he'd been holding it in the whole time. A mixture of awe and

---

[7] *The Little Prince*, by Antoine de Saint-Exupéry.

relief, but also a strange kind of emptiness swirled in the pit of his stomach. Would he ever get this kind of absolution for the terrible thing he had done with his skill?

CHAPTER 19 *Settling Debts*

Ben stared at the horse and the teen, heart bulging from an unexpected mixture of feelings swirling inside.

I'm going home!

But he was going home for all the wrong reasons. He was going home because he had forced Sadalbari into submission, something he had never intended to do. And although he longed more than anything to see his mother and Mesmo, he suddenly found himself thinking of Hakim, Abdul and Nutmeg. Would he ever see them again? Would he have time to say goodbye?

Someone spoke in Arabic behind him. *"Wonderful! Wonderful!"* they said.

Ben whirled, the skill bursting awake from

the roots of his hair to the tip of his feet.

Sheikh Azhar and his interpreter came up beside him. A satisfied smile spread on Sheikh Azhar's face, and he lifted his hands in wonder at the scene unfolding before him. His dark blue tunic brushed against Ben's cheek as he did so. The bulky man with his red-and-white checkered head-dress watched Zayed gently coax the horse towards the stables. Sadalbari obliged, following the teen obediently.

Tense as an ice-pick, Ben opened his mouth, and Arabic words tumbled out. *"Is that the life you want for Zayed, too? Obedient and always fulfilling your will?"*

The Sheikh and the interpreter's heads snapped towards him in unison. A mixture of insult and surprise spread on their faces, but surprise won over.

Chills travelled up and down Ben's spine. *WHAT just happened?*

The interpreter stared at Ben like he had just pulled a bunny out of a hat. "Fascinating," he said in English. "You are a fast learner of languages." His eyes narrowed in mistrust. "Unless you were already versed in fluent Arabic before you came here?" He nodded to himself as if he'd reached the correct conclusion. "Unexpected," he mulled, then turned to the Sheikh to chat about what had just happened.

Ben's ears buzzed. Spiders crawled up his neck. He hadn't even noticed he had spoken Arabic. It had come naturally. Did it have something to do with what had happened last night? Had he triggered the skill to become something bigger, something mightier? Could it be that he was now capable of understanding the languages of all living things?

The idea was mind-boggling. The alien skill coursed through him like it was electricity, and he, a transmission tower—like it was alive, and he was just the recipient. Even worse, it was as if a deadly nuclear reactor had suddenly become exposed within him, and he had no idea what might trigger an explosive chain reaction.

He swallowed.

The interpreter whispered in Sheikh Azhar's ear, and the Sheikh turned to look straight at Ben for the very first time. He spoke in Arabic. *"You are a great horse whisperer. You have done my bidding, and I will heed your words. I thank you deeply for your services and, in exchange, I offer you one of my horses. I will abide by your choice."*

Ben's eyes widened. *"You want to give me a horse?"* He was unable to put a damper on the skill. The words came out fluid, which terrified him because he felt he was losing control again.

The interpreter jumped in, in English. "The Sheikh's purebreds are some of the finest in the land. Your choice will honour him."

"Nutmeg!" Ben whispered.

"I am sorry?"

Ben turned to him. "I want Nutmeg."

The interpreter frowned, and he and the Sheikh exchanged words, confused by Ben's choice. Finally, the Sheikh shrugged. The interpreter said to Ben, "Uh, yes, of course. Nutmeg is yours."

Ben's heart skipped a beat.

The interpreter took over. "Also, Sheikh Azhar bin-Rahman understands the value of your ability and, therefore, he remits to you a due payment of half a million dollars. This sum will be transferred to your bank account at once."

Ben's jaw dropped. "Half a million dollars?" he burst.

The interpreter looked troubled. "Is the fee too low?"

"What? No! Wait a minute! I don't want the Sheikh's money. I will not accept it!" How could he accept money for breaking Sadalbari? It felt all wrong. Why hadn't they proposed this from the start, instead of resorting to kidnapping schemes?

The interpreter's face paled as if he had never had anyone deny money given by the Sheikh before. "Refusing due payment by the Sheikh would be an unpardonable offence. This is not something that can be undone. The Sheikh's offer is irrevocable..."

"Then give it to Hakim," Ben blurted.

"Uh, excuse me?"

"The money. I don't want it. So give it to Hakim." It would help the trainer with his many children. Hakim needed financial support more than Ben did.

The interpreter gulped visibly as the Sheikh requested a translation. Ben turned, crossed his arms and shut his eyes, focusing on the ringing in his ears.

How was he supposed to control the skill now? It flowed like water from a broken tap. What if it burst out again like last night? How was he supposed to stop it, then?

It took some time for the Sheikh and the interpreter to go over Ben's offer. So long, in fact, that Ben turned to face them again. The Sheikh's eyes had become wider as he began to understand Ben's request. *"Hakim?"* he asked for the third time, to which the interpreter nodded.

The Sheik's eyes bulged, then he threw back his head and let out a howl of laughter.

Ben's cheeks turned a fiery crimson.

What's so funny?

Now he wished he *had* listened in to their conversation.

Even the interpreter joined in, laughing heartily as soon as he realized that laughing was permitted.

Unable to hide his grin, the Sheikh hiccupped. *"Hakim? Yes, Hakim, then. The money will go to Hakim..."* Both men chortled, as they turned and left Ben standing there, utterly baffled.

CHAPTER 20 *Left Behind*

Ben took one last look at the empty arena, then headed to his room. Servants bustled about, covering furniture, lowering blinds, and bringing suitcases to the lobby. Ben guessed he wasn't the only one leaving.

"Pack your bags, whisperer," Zayed had said as if Ben had mountains of belongings to stuff in multiple suitcases.

His hair and the folds of his tunic were full of sand from the night's events, so he took a long shower, pulled on his jeans and white t-shirt and ate the lunch Abdul must have left him while he was at the arena. The jeans felt scratchy and thick after having worn the light tunic for so long.

Ben yawned, his eyelids suddenly feeling

like lead. The emotions of the previous night and the uncontrolled use of the skill had left him drained. He'd lie down for a bit while he waited for the servants to finish their packing. He closed his eyes.

It only felt like a second.

Silence startled him. His eyelids flew open. Not a single sound came from outside the bedroom door. He leapt out of bed and glanced out the window to find dawn breaking. Had he really slept the whole afternoon and night away?

Ben gulped. This unrestrained use of the skill really messed up his energy levels.

Anxious to get going, Ben reached for his hoodie in the closet. Something slithered out of it.

"Aah!" he yelped, jerking back. "Echis!" *What on Earth are you doing here?*

The snake wrapped itself into a corner. *I deccide I sstay with you. You keep me ssafe.*

You decide? Uh, no, you don't! That's a very bad idea.

The snake's body unfurled as it slid towards Ben. *Pleasse?*

Ben wanted to scold the snake but somehow couldn't bring himself to do so. *Echis, you are safer in the desert than with me. The desert is your home; you'd be unhappy anywhere else.*

I happy withh you. I sstay.

Ben shook his head disapprovingly. He couldn't very well let Abdul find the venomous viper in his room, so he figured he'd carry it outside and have a serious talk with it.

Come on.

He attached his sweater around his waist and invited Echis into its hood. The snake snuggled up in the folds.

Nicce and warm here.

Yeah, well, don't get used to it.

Car engines roared to life in the distance. Ben froze. The cars revved up as if they were driving away.

Wait a minute! Fear grasped Ben's chest. *Are they leaving without me?*

He flung open the bedroom door, rushed down the corridor and burst into the entrance hallway. There had been a lot of activity while he slept: sofas had been pushed aside, the suitcases were gone, and two backpacks lay forgotten on the floor.

Ben rushed outside in time to watch a procession of cars, most with tinted windows, roll out of the driveway. A couple of bodyguards slipped into the last car. The interpreter's voice drifted toward him from a rolled-down window.

Ben's jaw dropped. "Hey!" he yelled, rushing up to the car. "Where are you going? What about me?'

The interpreter bent forward and said something, but the only word Ben could make out as the car rolled away was *'Hakim'.* Then the sound of laughter.

"What? Hey! Wait!" Ben couldn't believe it. He stumbled after the car as it sped off. Flabbergasted, he watched as the procession floated into the shimmering horizon, leaving him behind.

He sprinted around the driveway, convinced there must be one last car parked around a corner for him, but found none. He rushed inside, heart squeezing. Had Zayed lied? Had the Sheikh's son been toying with him about going home? Maybe this was some kind of rebuttal for last night's humiliation...

Ben's feet couldn't carry him fast enough down the corridor. He reached Zayed's appartement. No-one was there. The computers were gone.

He searched the kitchen, the large dining-room, the swimming pool. Not a soul in sight. A camel snorted under a palm tree by the oasis. He ran to it and found a couple of men tending to their goats. But they didn't have answers to his frantic questions.

Ben whirled, breathing heavily.

The stables!

They wouldn't leave the horses, would they?

On he went, crashing through the stable doors and making the horses neigh in surprise. He rushed to the other end and opened Sadalbari's stall.

The stallion scrambled back in utter panic, sensing Ben's skill sleeping under the surface. Ben stepped back, dismayed by the horse's reaction, but also deeply worried to find it unattended. After everything Sadalbari had been through, they had just left him behind like a broken toy.

Nutmeg! Where has everybody gone?

Nutmeg shook her mane. *They come, they go. The Sheikh has many properties. This is just one of them. They used to take me with them when Zayed was smaller, and he used to mount me. Now, I remain here. They send someone back to take care of us.*

But, but... Zayed promised...

Promised what, Benjamin? Zayed is not one to make promises.

Ben staggered back, his head swooning.

What did he promise you, Benjamin?

Ben wasn't sure he had it in him to answer. *He promised I could go home.*

Nutmeg munched on some straw, answering, *I don't know anything about that.*

Ben closed his eyes. *That's it, then.*

That's what?

I'm leaving, Nutmeg. I'm going to Dubai. I'll make it across the desert, somehow.

Nutmeg stopped munching. *You can't do that. You'll be long dead before you get there.*

Ben held his breath. *I have no choice.*

Fine, then. I'm coming with you.

Ben shook his head. *No, Nutmeg. I wanted you to come with me, but not like this. I can't ask you to do this for me.*

Nutmeg snorted. *You didn't ask. I'm telling you: I'm coming with you. Now get me out!*

Ben hesitated.

The horse stared at him with her large, black eyes. *Benjamin, I mean it. I'm coming, too.*

Feeling numb, Ben opened Nutmeg's stall. When he gently rested his skill onto Nutmeg's mind, he knew for certain that the horse understood what she was getting herself into, and yet she chose to come anyway.

Speechless at the horse's decision, Ben followed her to the riding gear, where Nutmeg explained how to saddle her. Then, he emptied the two forgotten backpacks from the main entrance and filled them with water bottles, flatbread, and anything else he could find. At the last minute, he remembered to grab a handful of sugar cubes for Nutmeg.

By the time he was done, it was late afternoon. He joined Nutmeg on the driveway and clambered on her back with some effort. Using a saddle was a completely different experience, but he would need to quickly get used to it.

Can we go now? Nutmeg snorted impatiently, making Ben smile.

Yes, Nutmeg, we can go.

He glanced back at the detailed entrance of the Sheikh's estate, realizing this would be the last time he'd lay eyes on it. As Nutmeg trotted across the circular driveway, Ben noted that the central fountain had been switched off. He'd been left behind, for sure.

Rage turned into determination, and he clicked his tongue. "Let's get out of here, Nutmeg."

A shout startled him.

"Sabi[8]!"

Ben turned to find Abdul running after him.

---

[8] Sabi = Arabic for "boy"

The man scolded him, waving his arms about and indicating he should get off the horse at once.

"No, Abdul. Not this time," Ben said.

Nutmeg side-stepped the man's movements so he could not pull Ben off her back.

"Let's go, Nutmeg."

The horse trotted away.

Ben thought Abdul would run after them, but instead, the man remained by the fountain. *"Stop! You must wait for me!"* Abdul shouted.

Ben frowned, then told Nutmeg to stop. It was alarming how easily the skill translated Abdul's words to him.

The chaperone disappeared inside, and for a minute, Ben worried that Abdul wanted to go with him. He was about to leave when Abdul reappeared with a blanket in his arms. He rushed to hand it over to Ben.

Ben didn't know why he needed a blanket in this heat, but he appreciated that Abdul was no longer trying to hold him back. The chaperone's rapid blinking and sweat on his brow told him he wished he could, though.

Ben's throat went dry, but he had no choice. He had to leave, or he'd wither away at the property, like one of Zayed's forgotten toys. *"Goodbye, Abdul. And thank you,"* he said.

Abdul blinked, his pained eyes a sign of deep worry. *"You stay, sabi. Master orders it. You die out there,"* he begged.

Master orders it, huh?

Ben let out a shaky breath. He set his jaw and led Nutmeg out through the golden gates of the estate.

CHAPTER 21 *Into the Desert*

Afternoon turned to night, and although a faint splash of light from Dubai illuminated the distant horizon, Ben was relieved that they had a road to follow in the dim light. Not a single car passed them by, nor did they see a single house or shed along the way, to the point where Ben wondered if the Sheikh had had this road built for his personal purpose.

Nutmeg shuddered. She had been doing this occasionally, ever since they had left, and Ben worried the horse was having second thoughts.

Are you okay, Nutmeg?

I'd feel better if you'd left that sneaky viper behind.

Ben started, suddenly remembering Echis.

Oh, right, Nutmeg! Sorry!

He pulled the snake from the folds of his hoodie. *Echis, it's time for me to let you go. You do realize you're a venomous snake, don't you?*

I not bite. Only if you sstare at me. Sstaring makess me edg...

All right, all right! Staring makes you edgy. I get it. The point is, my family and friends don't know that, and they'll step on you before I even get a chance to explain.

I not bite friendss and family. You protectss me. I good ssnake.

Ben snorted, but then felt bad because he truly believed the snake. *I don't know, Echis. What do you think, Nutmeg?*

Nutmeg huffed. *You know what I think.*

Ben sighed. *Look, you can travel with us for a bit, but when we get to the outskirts of Dubai, I'm letting you go, is that clear?*

Echis' hiss sounded deeply disappointed. *Yess, Benjamin.* And with that, the snake slid back into its makeshift home.

This time it was Ben's turn to shudder. *It's getting cold, isn't it?*

The desert turns cold at night. Sand does not release heat. Why don't you use the blanket?

Ben gasped. Abdul's blanket! He pulled it

over his shoulders, welcoming the warmth, and silently thanked his chaperone for looking after him once again.

The night wore on, stars shifted in the sky, and the road continued, unchanging, as if they were walking in one spot without moving forward.

The endless hours dragged by, and Ben felt drowsiness settle in. Unaccustomed to the saddle, he had to step down from time to time, not only to stay awake but because his backside hurt like crazy. He thought of asking Nutmeg to take a quick rest, but he didn't know how many hours remained of their trip, and he felt it was his responsibility to get Nutmeg to a place with water and shelter as soon as possible.

By daybreak, he could barely keep his eyes open. He hunched on Nutmeg's back, head drooping, the first rays of the sun on his arm a warning sign of the coming swelter. Within a few short hours, both Ben and Nutmeg were smothered in heat.

Nutmeg stopped. *I need a break.*

Ben slid off the horse's back in relief, landing flat on the ground when his numb legs would not carry him.

Nutmeg snorted in warning. *Our trip has barely started, Benjamin...*

I know, I know. I'm totally fine. My foot just missed the stirrup, is all.

Nutmeg didn't reply but gladly accepted water and food that Ben gave her, before he himself emptied half a water bottle in one gulp and chomped down on a flatbread.

Without a word, Ben limped to a taller dune and boy and horse settled in its shadow.

I'm just going to rest for a bit...

Ben barely had time to finish the sentence when he fell into a deep sleep.

Wake up, Benjamin. Nutmeg nudged him.

"What?" Ben gasped, sitting in a hurry. A headache throbbed at the back of his head. The noon sun beat down on them mercilessly. There was no hiding in the shadow of a dune, now.

He got up, muscles aching, and a fearsome doubt seeped into his mind. How much farther would they have to go? He gave Nutmeg some more water. "Let's go," he said, shoving the fear to the back of his mind. It couldn't be that much farther, could it?

By the time night fell once more, Ben knew they had reached a point of no return. Their only hope lay ahead.

Ben tried to ask a passing falcon to give him a bird's eye view of the area, but his head throbbed too much, his thoughts were jumbled, and he could barely talk to Nutmeg. He held on as long as he could, then yelped when he lost his balance and slid off Nutmeg's back.

Nutmeg tried to tell him something, but all he could do was shiver from the pain in his back, which was worsened by the rapidly falling temperature. Nutmeg nibbled at the blanket with her teeth to cover up Ben. He fished out a couple of sugar cubes from his jeans pocket for her.

He thought he would never be able to rest, yet when he opened his eyes, morning had broken. The motor of a car rumbled in the distance.

Ben rolled on to his stomach. "Nutmeg!" he called, noticing a cloud of sand lifted by a car in the distance.

It is the Sheikh.

Ben's stomach twisted. *Are you sure?*

My eyes are not good, but my ears would recognize that sound anywhere.

Quick, then! We have to hide.

Climbing the nearest dune turned into a nightmarish effort, but they made it over the crest in time to hide from the passing car. Ben watched as the long, black limousine dashed by with frustrating speed, heading in the direction of the

Sheikh's property.

Nutmeg, we've got to reach Dubai before they come back.

Ben regarded his friend worriedly as Nutmeg huffed through her nostrils.

Are you okay?

Are you?

Boy and horse looked at each other without answering. Ben fed Nutmeg the last supplies of food. He tried to ignore the dangerously low level of water, still convinced Dubai could not be that much further off.

Time to move on.

Ben wanted to make as much headway as they could, clasping onto the vague hope that they would reach some kind of shelter before the noon sun scorched them alive.

He gritted his teeth and blinked away stinging tears as he pulled himself on to Nutmeg's back. *Come on, Nutmeg, we can do this.*

But they couldn't.

Noon came and went. Even by the side of the road, the asphalt gave off such torrid temperatures that Ben was convinced they'd be roasted by the end of the day. A scorching wind slapped pinpricks of sand against his cheeks. He gave up trying to remove grains of sand that crunched between his teeth and coated his lips. His brain drifted into a mish-mash of visions, where mirages that resembled modern buildings lingered just out of arm's reach.

He found himself talking sluggishly to Mesmo at times and thought they were moving forward, but in a brief flicker of lucidity, he realized Nutmeg had almost come to a standstill.

Ben did not remember falling off the horse, but when he opened his eyes, the sun shone relentlessly.

"N'tmg." He tried to call his friend's name but found his tongue swollen and dry. His lips had become thick and cracked.

He turned his head and found Nutmeg lying in the sand, not far off. He flinched with worry, but a shadow fell over him, protecting him. Now the horse stood beside him, sheltering him from the rays of the sun.

They were confusing, these hallucinations. One second, Nutmeg was lying, drained, in the sand; the next, the white horse was shielding him from the elements.

Wait a minute... White horse... White...?

Ben stared. *Sadalbari?*—It was easy to talk to a hallucination—*I'm so sorry. I didn't mean to hurt you. I am responsible for you, but you fear me.*

Sadalbari's head filled Ben's eyesight. *Yes, I fear you. But you are not responsible for me.*

Ben blinked, confused. *But I broke you!*

Sadalbari puffed air out of its nostrils. *You cannot break the King of the Desert. Please, Master, set me free. Do not hold me back with your powers.*

Ben's heart broke at being called Master by the mighty stallion. *Of course, Sadalbari. You were never mine to keep. You will always be free.*

Ben reached out his hand to see if the horse was really there, but the stallion melted into the blinding sun.

A car revved up to his side. A black limousine.

Car doors opened. Cold air seeped out from inside. A dark blue robe swung before his face.

"Stupid, stupid boy," a bearded face said, the man's red-and-white checkered head-dress brushing against his cheek as he leaned in to lift Ben from the ground.

Ice-cold air washed over Ben from the car's air conditioning, a leather seat brushed against his cheek.

"N'meg," he cried with a last shred of energy.

As he drifted into a black hole of

unconsciousness, Ben wondered sadly if he would ever see home again.

* * *

Four days! Four days had passed, and Mesmo still hadn't found a single clue as to Einar's whereabouts. And the longer it took him to find Einar, the more Ben was slipping away from him. The thought was unbearable. He clenched his teeth until his jaw hurt.

Santorini in Greece, Mount Vesuvius and Mount Etna in Italy, Eyjafjallajökull in Iceland. He'd searched these four volcanoes from top to bottom.

Now he was headed for the fifth location circled on Einar's map: Beerenberg, an active volcano on the island of Jan Mayen, tucked away in a lonely spot of the Northern Atlantic Ocean.

Mesmo had little hope left. His trails were going cold, and Inspector Hao had not uncovered anything new regarding the plane that had landed in the Canary Islands. Their search for Ben was nearing a dead-end.

He scanned the island of Jan Mayen with the spaceship's scanners and found half-a-dozen buildings on its southern side, located far from the volcano. He set down the spaceship and observed the few comings-and-goings of a handful of people.

Judging from the strange apparatus sticking out from the rooftops, this was not a town or village but rather, a scientific and meteorological outpost. From here, the island's weather and volcanic activity could be studied. It was the type of place Einar would have frequented as a volcanologist.

When nothing appeared to be suspicious, Mesmo travelled to the massive volcano, which was shrouded in mist and snow. This made visibility poor, and he was about to give up when he spotted a tiny square building nestled in a rugged portion of the mountain's flank.

Mesmo landed not far from it, the jagged slope making it hard to find a stable area for the spaceship. When he exited the craft, a strong gust of freezing wind slapped him in the face. Snowflakes swirled around him. He used his water skill to shield himself from the Arctic-type weather, stepped into the snow, and approached the small building.

The door was locked, so he used the surrounding snow to freeze the lock until it broke. The door blew inward.

Mesmo stepped inside and found himself in a square space the size of a bedroom. The back wall was made of solid mountain rock. The room was filled with machinery that buzzed and zoomed, taking automatic and constant measurements of the mountains and weather, probably sending signals to the outpost he'd seen further south.

Disappointed, Mesmo was about to leave when he spotted what he was looking for: a symbol resembling a treble clef from a music partition, carved into the rock. He instantly recognized the Toreq sign. Heart racing, he rushed to touch the symbol.

A hidden door slid to the side, revealing a dark tunnel that went straight into the mountain. Hot air carrying a smell of sulphur hit him in the face, making him cringe. His skill did not do well in surroundings devoid of water, and he felt it retract from his skin.

Mesmo stared into the darkness, spiders crawling up and down his spine.

A trap!

He could feel it. He stepped back and wiped the cold sweat from his brow.

But what if Ben's in there?

His stomach constricted at the idea. He had

no choice. He knew he had to go in.

First, he stepped back outside, placed his hand in the snow, and sent water streaming into the tunnel with his skill. He bathed the rocky walls with the liquid, turning them to shimmering ice. Then, he tore off a large piece of the weather apparatus and placed it in the doorway so it wouldn't close in on him.

Mesmo stared into the gloom again. The glow from his hands reflected on the ice so that it illuminated the tunnel some way down. Bracing himself, he stepped into the gloom, listening to his breath echoing off the rocky wall. The smell of humid steam reached his nostrils. The ice was melting in the rising heat, and he had trouble maintaining it in place.

The tunnel went on and on until he reached a dead end.

Another door.

The same symbol.

He waved his hand over it. The door slid open.

Sensor-activated lights flickered on beyond, revealing a highly sophisticated room filled with screens and machinery. On the far side of the room, a wide window looked out into darkness. Stifling heat within the room made it hard to think, and Mesmo's attempts to maintain an icy surface around the tunnel faltered. Fortunately, a ventilation system kicked into action, extracting some of the thick air.

Mesmo scanned the room without moving from the doorway but found the space empty. No Einar, no Ben. Yet he froze in place because his eyes had fallen on something he had not expected—something he thought he would never see again in his lifetime.

The screens within the room were not man-made. They were Toreq. And a vertical beam that emanated from one of them indicated there was a message—a *Toreq* message!

Catching his breath and ignoring the hot, fetid air, he rushed to the screen, swiped over the beam, and watched streams of symbols unfold before him. A green outline of the planets of the Solar System expanded across the room, accompanied by metallic voices that echoed around him like a ghostly presence.

Then, just as the image focused on Earth, the message wavered and vanished. As if on cue, the sensor-activated lights switched off, plunging the room into darkness. And behind him, Mesmo heard the door slide closed.

He flung himself in its direction, stumbling

over machinery, and grabbed whatever loose object he could find. His hand closed on what felt like a dismantled computer panel. He swung it through the door at the last second. The metal bent in resistance as the heavy door shut on it, but it did not break.

The low, whirring sound from the ventilation system switched off. Mesmo panted, sweat pearling his forehead. A sliver of air entered through the crack above the computer panel, but that was it. Grunting under the effort, he pulled at the opening with the tip of his fingers, but they wouldn't fit through the crack. He pulled at the panel, hoping the door would give, but instead, the panel threatened to tear apart.

The torrid room was affecting his skill, making him weak. It withdrew within him, seeking protection like a mollusk shutting itself in its shell.

Sagging back, Mesmo stared at the room and froze. It wasn't as dark as he'd initially thought. An eerie, pulsating glow reflected against the walls. It came from the window.

Pulling himself to his feet, Mesmo headed to the window and leaned his forehead against it. On the other side, an endless pit forged in solid rock within the heart of the mountain tumbled into a river of thick, red magma far below.

CHAPTER 22 *Kindred Spirits*

Ben woke up in a hospital. No more sand, endless dunes or scorching sun.

I'm alive!

That single thought sent him into a soothing sleep again.

The next time Ben stirred, a nurse was switching a port in his arm. He wanted to sit up, but his head swayed so hard he had to lie back. She pushed him back gently, and he drifted off once more.

The third time he came to, his mind felt much sharper. A food tray lay on a table beside him. To his right, bright light came in from a large window. Skyscrapers cut through the view outside.

A man seated next to the bed stood, startling

him. The man with a dark blue tunic and red-and-white checkered head-dress approached the window and closed the see-through curtains, dimming the sharp light from outside, for which Ben was grateful.

The man returned to his seat. He leaned forward and said, "Stupid, stupid boy."

Ben gasped. *"Hakim?"* He stared at the familiar face, then winced at the large blister he felt on his lip. The horse trainer smiled, his tired eyes becoming sombre. "I very angry with you. You stupid boy. You almost die. Why you leave? Why you not wait for me?"

Ben gaped.

Wait for him?

Was Hakim supposed to pick him up at the Sheik's home? He remembered the Sheik's interpreter saying something about Hakim before driving off. And Ben had thought he had been making some kind of joke at his expense. "You... you were going to pick me up...?" he spoke the words slowly.

Hakim nodded. "I offer Sheikh Azhar to take you to airport. He agree. I arrive at estate. Find Abdul in panic. Say you leave into desert. Very, very stupid." His stern gaze fell on Ben.

"Aah..." Ben said slowly, suddenly feeling

very foolish—as in crawl-under-the-ground foolish. Heat rose to his cheeks as he realized his terrible mistake. And all because he'd refused to use his skill to listen in on the Sheikh and the interpreter's conversation. He'd been too quick to judge Zayed. The teen hadn't lied to him. The Sheikh hadn't lied to him. They had promised him that he could go home once he'd fulfilled his task...

He swallowed hard, remembering the unforgiving sun, the hallucinations, Nutmeg lying in the sand...

He jolted upright. "Hakim, what about Nutmeg?" he blurted, wincing at his painful lip.

Hakim's face softened. "Nutmeg fine. Strong horse. Recover quickly."

"Oh, good!" Ben breathed in relief. He closed his eyes to let the good news sink in. He'd never have forgiven himself if something had happened to Nutmeg.

He opened his eyes again and stared at the horse trainer. There was something different about him. "Hakim, why are you dressed like that? You look... different."

Hakim smiled. He placed a hand on his heart. "I, Sheikh Hakim Sulayman."

"Huh?" Ben blinked. He knew he should stop

staring, but he couldn't help himself. *"Sheikh...?"*

Hakim nodded. "I brother-in-law of Sheikh Azhar bin-Rahman. Azhar and I, friends since little boys. Grow up together. Great happiness in family when Azhar marry my sister." His face fell. "But then Sadalbari kill my sister and everything change."

Ben's head spun.

Hakim gestured towards himself. "Azhar and I, important business-men in country. Always busy, always travelling. Much responsibility.

"But when I with horse, I true self. When I horse trainer, I calm. No pressure from business, from responsibilities. Just me and horse. I not need to talk. I at peace." He placed a hand on Ben's own. "So you know real Hakim. Not Sheikh, not businessman. Just Hakim, horse lover, like you. You understand?"

Ben did, and it made him smile shyly. He rested his head on the cushion, amazed and overwhelmed. His friend, Hakim: a Sheikh!

He loved the way Hakim paid extra attention to the person he was talking to, or the task he was accomplishing as if nothing else mattered in that moment. It made Ben feel special. He vowed to be more like that, too.

But then the blush returned to his cheeks,

turning scarlet this time. "Uh... so... uh... I guess you don't really need any money?"

No wonder Sheikh Azhar and his interpreter had thought his idea of giving money to the horse trainer was hilarious.

Hakim chuckled, but not in a mocking way. "Azhar tell me you give money to me. I grateful for offer, but I not need money." He bent to fish something out of a briefcase by his chair. "You not want money; I not want money. So, I find solution. I donate money to big cause. Important non-profit organization." He handed Ben a tablet.

Ben stared at the website that lay open before him. Several videos displayed interviews he had given recently, as well as pictures of newspaper clippings. There were videos and articles about animals as well. Ben stared at the website's name and caught his breath: *great-gathering.org*. It was the website Kimi and his friends had created for him.

In the center of the website, the general flow of information was interrupted by a single picture. It was a photograph of his face, and on top of it, in bold, red letters, were the words: HAVE YOU SEEN BEN?

Ben slumped back and shut his eyes. It took him a while before he could open them again.

Hakim was pulling something else from his briefcase. He handed Ben a passport and first-class plane ticket. "You rest. Get strong for flying tomorrow morning. You go home, do important work. When you need help, you call Hakim. You call Azhar. We business-men with great influence. We help your cause." He paused. "Azhar and his son too proud to admit they sorry. Azhar ashamed his son take you from your home. Very angry with Zayed. Could have caused big diplomatic problem. Not good for business."

Ben gasped. So it had been Zayed all along who had been behind his kidnapping... Zayed's word echoed in his brain: *Misbehaving is the only way I can get my father's attention.*

No wonder Sheikh Azhar had seemed so grumpy on their first encounter.

Hakim continued, "When Azhar realize his son's bad act, he secretly hope maybe you tame Sadalbari after all, then he can send you home with big sum of money. As way of thanks."

Ben thought about that for a minute. Weird way of saying sorry. Now he understood Zayed's relationship with his father better, too. It seemed to be a habit of the Sheikh's to distribute wealthy gifts. Maybe it was easier than actually talking about his feelings. "What about you?" he asked, turning to the horse trainer. "Couldn't you have done something?"

Hakim sat back and sighed. "I never meddle in Azhar's affairs. Not my place. Azhar never dream of meddling with me or my family. That is unspoken rule between us. All I can do is watch, make sure you okay, Zayed okay. Report to Azhar. Azhar come as soon as he could when he hear Sadalbari try to trample you. He and Zayed have big fight."

Ben crossed his arms over his chest. "You know why Zayed is misbehaving like this, don't you?" he asked.

Hakim smiled and let Ben explain.

"He's just trying to get his dad's attention. He feels lonely and misses his dad. He doesn't care about expensive gifts. All he wants is to spend some time with his dad. And..." Ben added, "I think he wants to become an artist, but his dad won't let him."

Hakim's eyes twinkled. He rubbed his chin and said, "Then, I right. You great whisperer indeed. You bring peace between horse and rider. You bring peace between father and son."

Ben blushed. "What do you mean?" he asked, releasing his crossed arms.

"When Sheikh Azhar leave desert estate,

Zayed run after car and insist on riding with him. Father and son talk all the way to Dubai. Now, they are at ocean property. They talk many days together without fighting. Zayed has agreed to take over family company. Sheikh Azhar has agreed to display son's art all over world. They will do this together."

"Really? Wow!"

"Zayed very clever. Very capable of managing business. But he must still learn to calm his wild soul."

Ben tried to smile through his stinging blister. "It sounds like Zayed's going to have his hands full."

Hakim nodded in agreement. "That good thing. Keep his mind busy. No room for mischief."

Ben grinned.

They stared at each other in silence for a moment, and Ben knew this was goodbye.

Hakim took his briefcase and stood. "I deeply sorry for what happen to you. I hope, one day, you able to forgive. You welcome at my home anytime, ride horses, visit Dubai." He pointed to the tablet. "You keep device and call family now. Yes?"

Ben looked at the tablet. "Thank you, Hakim," he said, suddenly feeling gloomy. "I'll miss you."

Hakim's face faltered. "I miss you, too, *sabi*." He bowed his head and stepped towards the door.

"Hakim," Ben called after him. "What about Sadalbari? Who is going to take care of him?"

A look of confusion crossed the man's eyes. "Ah, you not know then," he said. "Zayed come back with me to pick you up at property. When we arrive, Zayed offer Sadalbari a choice: to stay or to go. Stallion run off into desert, like you." He thought for a moment, then added, "We humans always want to own things, even living things. Put animals in zoos, tame them for shows. Many men would wish to own the legendary King of Horses. I proud of Zayed. It take him great courage and wisdom to set free something he wishes to own. Wild things must remain wild. Our duty is to observe wilderness from a distance, without interfering."

Ben's eyes widened as the man spoke, a faint hope rising in his chest. "Somehow, I feel like Zayed and Sadalbari are kindred spirits."

Hakim nodded. "As I believe perhaps are you and I," he said, smiling at Ben.

Ben beamed.

"You not feel sad for what you did to Sadalbari," Hakim continued. "You did right thing;

saved Zayed's life. And Zayed has learned to set free what must stay wild. Never forget that."

Ben let out a shaky breath, overwhelmed that Hakim had such a clear idea of his inner torment. He nodded. He'd try to remember.

Hakim smiled his usual peaceful smile. "I honoured to meet you, Benjamin Archer. May Allah guide your steps."

"Goodbye, Hakim," Ben said through a lump in his throat.

CHAPTER 23 *Revelation*

Nothing made sense any more. Minutes turned into hours, hours into days. Mesmo came to and coughed. His nostrils, imbued with the smell of sulphur, burned his airway.

He turned his head. The dark room swayed before his eyes. Clothes drenched in sweat, he dragged himself back to the slit in the door, taking in a hungry gulp of air. The cool draft that came from the tunnel beyond filled his lungs but was not enough.

The skill had retracted deep within him, the pores of his skin filling with heat. Unbearable heat.

For the hundredth time, he tried to pull the door open, breaking another nail in the process. Black spots swam before his eyes, the room dipped to the side, and he fell into unconsciousness again.

* * *

Bright lights. Horrible, painful light that stabbed his eyes, followed by wonderful, cold air that filled his lungs. Mesmo breathed in so deep he had to roll to the side and retch. He coughed and coughed.

Rolling on his back again, his eyes tried to focus on the figure standing over him.

"Still breathing, I see," Einar said. The Norseman stared down at him with expressionless eyes, hands behind his back.

The ventilation system kicked into gear. Mesmo tried to stand, but his arms and legs wouldn't obey.

The corner of Einar's mouth curled into a smile. "You found my map," he stated. "Did you enjoy the sightseeing trip I sent you on?" he smirked. "I knew you would hate it, all that travelling to some of the planet's hottest spots, places devoid of water. It must be painful, being stripped of the very element that feeds your skill..."

Mesmo blinked, acutely aware that the door

was open. Wonderful oxygen coming from the tunnel reactivated his brain.

Einar noticed. He took a few steps back, waved his hand at a mechanism, and the door slid closed, trapping the thick heat inside, though the lights remained on. "Let's talk, shall we? For old time's sake..."

Mesmo struggled to stay conscious. "Where's Benjamin?" he croaked.

Einar stared at him from the doorway, one eyebrow raised. "Is that really what concerns you?" He straightened, looking thoughtful as if he were trying to figure out the answer to his own question. "Well, of course. Your heroic move to bring the boy back to Earth wouldn't mean much if he were lost to you, would it? How unfortunate, the great Toreq Observer, bearer of the Arch Council's most esteemed mission, turns his back on his people for the sake of a single A'hmun child—only to have the child disappear. Tragic, indeed!"

"Where is he?" Mesmo yelled, thrust into an uncontrollable bout of coughing.

Einar waited for him to calm down, then sighed. "Frankly, I don't know, and I don't care."

"You lie!"

Einar shrugged. "When the media reported

him missing, I figured you'd come looking for me." He strolled over to Mesmo. "I hate to disappoint you, but I don't have him. Someone beat me to it. Not that I'm surprised. When your little protégé revealed his Toreq skill to the media, who knows whose greedy eyes he attracted? But that's what you wanted, wasn't it? For us to expose ourselves to the world, spread our knowledge like seeds to the wind... And look where that got him."

Mesmo spat. "At least he's trying, which is more than you can say."

Einar's face tensed. "You worry about such little things, Mesmo. You forget the bigger picture. This is about millennia of enmity between the Toreq and the A'hmun. This is about two civilizations who almost blasted each other into oblivion. And it could happen again if the A'hmun are not contained. You and the boy's efforts are futile. You've run out of time."

Mesmo tried to get up again, but couldn't. He dragged himself next to the door and leaned against the wall in a half-sitting position, panting. His hand touched something humid on the floor. Einar had left muddy footprints upon entering the room, which meant the tunnel was still wet from the melted ice. "There is always time! And Benjamin's life is not meaningless!" Mesmo said, trying to figure out what to do about the wet tunnel behind the closed door. "Ben shows the spark of valour the Toreq have been looking for in the A'hmun since the end of the Great War of the Kins. He represents the very hope that my people clung to when they decided not to exterminate the A'hmun all those tens of thousands of years ago. The Toreq have always known, deep down, that that spark existed. Ben cares. And he's prepared to face all odds to reach real change, with or without the Toreq skill. If Benjamin exists, then others like him exist, too. You, as a Wise One, should realize the value in that better than anyone."

Einar stepped towards the window, hands folded in the small of his back, magma reflecting in red waves over his face. "I just told you, Mesmo. Your efforts are too little, too late. You have fallen on the wrong side of history. You will be remembered as the one who sided with the A'hmun against the Toreq."

"There are no sides, Einar!" Mesmo yelled. "Don't you get it? There don't *need* to be sides." He was sweating profusely, losing vital hydration.

Einar turned to him with a faraway look. "When you called the meeting of Wise Ones, I thought you already knew. Why else would you have called us? Imagine my surprise when it turned out you *didn't* know. Imagine my surprise when you exposed your plan to rebel against the Arch Council and asked us to do the same..."

Mesmo shook his head in frustration. "You speak in riddles, Einar."

Einar glared darkly at Mesmo. "Your treason forced me to act against my kin. You forced me to act against the rebellious Wise Ones."

A cold ripple travelled up Mesmo's spine. "You killed Su Tai and Akeya!" he breathed.

Einar turned to face the window again but didn't answer.

"Why, Einar? What is it I don't know?"

The Norseman stared out the window for a tense moment, then pulled something flat and circular out of his pocket. "Do you know what this is?"

Mesmo did. He recognized the Toreq device but said nothing.

Einar held it up, admiring it. "I placed this on your spaceship after our meeting. It blocks all incoming and outgoing communications." He headed for the Toreq screens, where Mesmo had previously watched the interrupted message.

Einar waved his hand, and the Solar System spread out once more over the room, outlined in green. The metallic voice turned into several metallic voices, indicating the messages came from several alien sources, and the image zoomed in towards the Sun. "I sent you sightseeing to stall you. But I figured, if you ever made it to this research room, you'd be attracted by this Toreq message. And I was right to set the trap. That said, I wouldn't want to leave without showing you the full message first."

The image skimmed by Mars, then headed towards Earth, approaching pinpoints of lights near the Moon. As the dots expanded, Mesmo watched them turn into five massive Toreq spaceships.

Not just any spaceships...

Mesmo gasped.

Warships!

"You see why it is too late?" Einar breathed, his voice sounding far away as he admired the dark crafts. He turned to Mesmo, his voice heavy with meaning. *"They are already here."*

Mesmo lunged at Einar. He reacted before he could think. But his limbs were weak, and the Norseman sidestepped his attack easily.

"Tsk, tsk," Einar said, opening the door again. "Accept the inevitable, Mesmo. See the bigger picture. The Arch Council has taken its position. They have sent in the Toreq warships.

The A'hmun are doomed. And anyone or anything that stands in their way must be eliminated. You sent the Wise Ones into hiding, which suits me fine. They won't even know what hit them. And you..." he paused. "I am sorry you made the wrong call, I truly am."

"Einar!" Mesmo said weakly. "Aren't you forgetting something?"

The Norseman turned, frowning. His feet splashed in the thin puddle of water. He noticed it too late.

Mesmo called forth his water skill, forcing it out of its shell from deep within him. He yelled under the strain, slapped his hand in the water and transformed it into ice. Einar's feet locked to the ground.

It wasn't much, but it was enough. By the time the Norseman reacted, Mesmo was already on his feet, throwing himself at Einar.

The two men fell heavily to the ground. Mesmo was too slow, the time spent in the stifling room having taken its toll. Einar hit him square in the chin. Mesmo hurtled back, seeing stars, while Einar scrambled to his feet, lunging for the door.

Frantic, Mesmo tripped Einar with his foot, sending the Norseman flat on his stomach half-in and half-out of the door, knocking the air out of him. Mesmo grabbed the bottom of Einar's trousers and dragged him back inside.

Einar rolled over and kicked Mesmo in the ribs. Mesmo wheezed but ignored the pain and pulled Einar towards him. The Norseman turned to attack. Still lying on the ground, Mesmo grabbed Einar by the shoulders and shoved him in the stomach with both feet—so hard that Einar somersaulted over Mesmo's head and crashed into the window.

A yelp was followed by exploding glass, then Einar vanished into the dark beyond.

Gasping, Mesmo crawled to the window, fighting to remain conscious as searing heat from the magma flow belched into the room. Einar lay in a heap on a ledge, some way below, unconscious. Though splatters of magma flowed through the deep mountain cavern below, they were too far down to put the Norseman in danger. He would survive.

Mesmo staggered back, his body screaming for air and water. Mesmo tumbled into the tunnel, his head swaying at the sudden onslaught of oxygen. He had to drag himself back up to reach the building and the outdoors. Once back on the mountain, he collapsed flat on his back in the snow. The contact with the cold made him cry out, the pores of his skin finally able to release the accumulated heat.

His cellphone rang in his pocket. The sound was like a lifeline in the waves of darkness that washed over him. Hands shaking, he struggled to pull out the phone. He blinked and focused on the twenty missed calls, then pressed the answer button.

"Mesmo!" Laura burst. "Where *are* you? I've been calling for hours. Inspector Hao has found Ben! He's safe and sound! He's in Dubai!"

Mesmo stared at the phone while snow swirled around him. His brain had trouble processing the news.

"Mesmo? Are you still there?"

"Laura!" he gasped, containing a groan of pain. He was still grappling with the enormity of Einar's earth-shattering revelation.

"Mesmo? What's wrong? Are you okay?"

"Laura!" he said. "Tell Ben *not to move!* Send me his location. I'm on my way to pick him up." He pressed the phone against his ear until it hurt. "Laura? Did you hear me? *Don't let him go anywhere!*"

There was a pause on the other end. "O-okay! Y-you don't sound good, Mesmo. W-what's going on?"

Mesmo picked himself up from the snow and staggered to the spaceship. "It's the Toreq, Laura! *The Toreq are here!*"

Silence on the other end.

"Laura?"

"I don't understand..."

"My people, *they are here!* With *warships!* Get ahold of Ben. Tell him I'll be there in a couple of hours. Tell him *not to move!* Do you understand?"

"Uh... Y-yes."

"Good! Ben and I will see you in a bit."

He hung up and leapt into the spaceship.

The Toreq woman who waited for him inside lifted her glowing hand. She struck Mesmo in the stomach with a force as great as lightning, knocking the air out of him and sending him tumbling into darkness.

CHAPTER 24 *Gifts*

Ben stared at the empty doorway for a long time, thinking of Sadalbari.

Maybe I didn't break him after all...

Sadalbari spoke to him from the back of his mind: *Release me, Master. Set me free.*

Had Sadalbari really protected him from the sun while he lay barely conscious by the side of the road? Or had he only imagined it in his feverishly dehydrated state?

Could it be that Sadalbari was still whole and wild? That Ben had managed to rein in the alien skill before it destroyed the stallion's mind? He gave a shaky sigh, realizing he may never know the answer.

His eyes fell on the tablet, and, on a hunch,

he Googled 'Sheikh Hakim Sulayman'. An impressive list of websites about his friend appeared. It turned out Hakim was the first businessman to back solar-powered energy in the country. There were pictures of him standing before endless rows of solar panels that were laid out in the sand, and in some pictures, he was shaking hands with Sheikh Azhar, who, the comments explained, promised to switch his company from oil extraction to green energy.

Ben then checked for Zayed but found nothing. He wondered if the teenager would one day be pictured with the two Sheikhs as a businessman or as an artist—or maybe both.

He dropped the tablet on his lap, realizing that he was stalling. Here he lay with a device in his hands which was connected to the internet, which meant he could call his mother...

He had waited so long for this that the moment felt surreal, and his heart raced faster as he pressed a social media app with trembling fingers.

The device rang.

Laura picked up instantly, and Ben almost fainted at the sight of her face on the screen.

"Ben!" she shrieked, then burst into tears.

Neither was able to speak for several

minutes.

"Are you okay?" she sobbed.

Ben nodded, unable to find his voice.

"Oh Ben, we were so distressed when we couldn't find you. We searched everywhere! Inspector Hao got his best people on your case, and Mesmo searched every corner of the Earth. But we never thought, it never occurred to us…" She broke off, her eyes wanting to tell a thousand stories, but her emotions stopping her from doing so.

"I'm f-fine, Mom, r-really. I'm in D-Dubai," Ben hiccupped.

She nodded. "Yes, I know. Inspector Hao just informed me. I was going to come on the first plane over, but Mesmo said not to." She gulped. "Ben, Mesmo is coming to pick you up. He'll be there in a couple of hours."

Ben gasped. "What? Are you kidding? With the *spaceship*?" Glancing at his plane ticket, he added, "Is that a good idea? I mean, shouldn't I be getting back home in a more 'normal' way?" He pictured Mesmo's spacecraft parking in front of the Dubai highrise.

Laura's face didn't reflect his enthusiasm. "Yes. We have no choice. He needs you home right away…" From the frown on her face, Ben knew she wanted to say more, but just then the doorbell rang. "Um... look, we'll talk about it when you get here. Just stay put. Don't go anywhere." While she spoke, she opened the front door, leaving Ben wondering if there was something she wasn't telling him.

"Hold on, Ben," Laura said, and he heard a man talk to her. Then two men wearing a delivery company uniform appeared on the screen, placing a flat cardboard box against the outside wall, then heading back to their delivery truck.

"What's that?" he asked, squinting at the screen.

"I don't know," Laura said. "But it says it's for you."

"For me?"

"Yeah. Hold on." She tore an opening in the cardboard. When she peeled back a corner, a painting appeared. "What's that?" Laura asked, stepping back so she could show him the full frame. "It's beautiful!"

Ben gasped.

The *Star Rider*!

It was Zayed's painting. The one with Sadalbari and Zayed's mother on the dunes. And it suddenly occurred to Ben why she was not riding the stallion in the painting. It was because Zayed's mother had always known Sadalbari would never be tamed, even if the stallion had briefly allowed her to mount him. Zayed must have sensed his mother and the horse's mutual respect, which was why he had drawn her beside it, not riding it. She was, in the end, Sadalbari's one true rider.

"There's a message," Laura said, pulling the torn page of a book stuck to the corner of the frame. She read an underlined passage aloud, *"To me, you are still nothing more than a little boy who is just like a hundred thousand other little boys. And I have no need of you. And you, on your part, have no need of me. To you I am nothing more than a fox like a hundred thousand other foxes. But if you tame me, then we shall need each other. To me, you will be unique in all the world. To you, I shall be unique in all the world.*[9]*"* She broke off and stared at the page.

Ben couldn't find his voice. The quote! It was the full quote from *The Little Prince*—the one about friendship... Was Zayed saying he considered Ben his friend?

"I..." Ben began, but Laura's exclamation cut him short. "Mom, what's going on?" Ben asked

---

[9] *The Little Prince* by French author Antoine de Saint-Exupéry

worriedly, hearing the disbelief in Laura's voice as she argued with the delivery employees.

Her green eyes burst on to the screen. "Ben, are you *kidding* me?" The device crackled as she spoke straight into the speaker. "Ben?" she almost sounded hysterical. "Did you get a *horse*?"

She adjusted the camera, and Ben watched as Nutmeg stepped out of the truck and trotted on to the lawn.

Ben's jaw fell to the ground. Then, unable to wipe a grin from his face, he threw back his head and laughed.

CHAPTER 25 *Unexpected Visitors*

"You need to get ready," Laura had said before hanging up. "Mesmo will pick you up in a couple of hours."

Ben's heart beat faster. *Mesmo's coming!* He couldn't believe it. And with the spaceship at that! A thrill travelled up his spine. This was finally happening! He couldn't wait!

Warmth spread through his body at the thought that Mesmo had found him worthy enough to risk pulling the spaceship from its hiding spot.

He pulled off the medical tubes from his arms and jumped off the bed... then almost crash-landed on the floor. His legs wouldn't hold him up.

Easy now!

This was no time for accidents. He'd dress slowly and have a bite to eat. There was time.

He waited until he felt strong enough, then held on to the side of the bed to help himself get to a narrow cupboard on the other side of the room. He opened it and caught his reflection in a mirror stuck to the inside of the door.

He stared.

Was that the same Ben Archer from before? How long had he been here? A dreadful thought crossed his mind. It couldn't be December yet, could it?

Don't be daft! Of course not!

It felt like it, though, but he knew he couldn't have been here more than a couple of weeks, at the most. Of course, it wasn't December, and of course, he hadn't missed The Great Gathering at the mouth of the Amazon River, he reassured himself.

That would've been terrible!

He stared at his ruffled hair, the dark pockets under his eyes, the ugly blister on his lower lip, his red-and-brown cheeks roasted by the sun, exposing some freckles. He pressed his hair flat, grains of sand on his scalp rubbing against the palm of his hand, then approached the mirror so he could look at his eyes.

Was that the skill lurking there, deep behind the brown of his iris? The skill that he had come to love, but which now troubled him once more?

He pulled back, stomach churning. He and Mesmo were going to need to have a very, very serious talk.

Ben glanced inside the cupboard and found his folded clothes and sandals on top of a box. His hoodie hung from a hook.

He picked up all the items and placed them on the bed, wondering what could be in the box. As he reached for the lid, something slid out of his sweater and plopped onto the bed.

"Yikes!" Ben yelled. *Echis!*

Echis rolled up on itself sheepishly. *Ssorry I sstartle you. I happy to ssee you. Are you happy to ssee me?*

Ben groaned. *Seriously, Echis. You have a way of getting around.*

Now I sstay withh you. Yess?

Ben slapped his face. *Nooo, Echis!*

The snake hid its head in its coils.

Ben rolled his eyes. *Think for a minute! You wouldn't be happy where I live. I mean, do you realize it SNOWS back home?*

What iss ssnow?

Agh! See what I mean? And, besides, I wouldn't even know what to feed you.

I not hungry. I eat plenty. Catch deliciouss mousse in dessert while you ssleep. Iss in belly. Ssee?

YUUUCK!

Ben gagged. He took off the hospital gown hurriedly, pulled on his jeans, t-shirt and hoodie, then stretched his arm towards the snake. *You get on over here before somebody sees you. I'm dropping you off in the desert, and that's final. Do you understand?*

Echis whimpered.

Ben snapped his fingers. *Come on, you silly snake!*

Sstop sstaring. I edgy when you ss...

Yes, yes, I know. He picked up the snake and dropped it into the hoodie of his sweater. *And no more whining!*

Ben stood still, expecting an answer. When none came, he puffed his cheeks, shook his head, and reached for the box again.

He lifted the lid and gasped.

The box contained a brand-new pair of black sneakers, identical to his old ones. He picked them up to admire them. Whoever had left them for him—Hakim, Azhar, or Zayed—sure knew what they were doing. He bent to try on the shoes and found that they fit perfectly.

His eyes fell on the sandals. He picked one up and felt the soft leather under his skin, then followed the shape of his foot imprinted on its surface. He'd gotten used to them.

I don't need sandals where I'm going, he reminded himself. He dropped the sandal on the bed with a sigh and bent to tie his shoelaces.

That's when he heard a scream.

He froze. The scream had come from down the hospital corridor. Had it been another patient?

Footsteps rushed by his room.

All senses alert, Ben lifted his head in time to watch two nurses run by. He finished tying his laces in a hurry, then stood with a beating heart. Terrified voices rose from another part of the ward.

What's going on?

A shadow fell over his room as if the sky had suddenly darkened from storm clouds outside.

Ben snapped his head towards the window to find that something was blotting out the sunlight. Rushing to the window, he flung the drapes aside.

Mesmo's spaceship hovered a few feet from his room. Sleek, black, and mysterious.

"MESMO!" Ben whooped, laughing and wincing at his sore lip all at once. *Already?*

Mesmo was making a spectacle of himself. He'd terrify half of Dubai if he stayed there long.

Instruments crashed to the ground down the ward, startling Ben. There were screams and running feet. Several people fled down the corridor, bypassing Ben's room as if chased by bloodhounds.

Jeez, Mesmo! Ben's heart almost beat out of his chest. This was so unlike him. Not stealthy and discreet at all.

Ben turned and raised his arms to wave at the spaceship, then froze. Blood drained from his face all the way down to his feet. Spiders crawled up and down his spine.

It wasn't one spaceship he was looking at, but two. Then a third slid down in formation beside the others. Three identical alien spacecraft, hovering before his window.

Ben gawked, eyes popping out of his head. Not one. Not two, but THREE spaceships!

How was that possible? He only knew of one spaceship, and that one belonged to Mesmo. He didn't know of any others.

He realized his arms were still raised in a weird, half-greeting. He dropped them slowly to his sides, a mind-boggling thought entering his brain.

That's not Mesmo! The words roared through his head like a tornado. *THAT'S NOT MESMO!* His thoughts scrambled all over each other. *But if that's not Mesmo, then WHO IS IT?*

Goosebumps rose on his arms, cold sweat trickled down his back, and a sudden urge to flee in panic like the others took hold of him.

He turned to face the door. A doctor shrieked at something he saw down the corridor. The doctor stumbled, picked himself up, and fled.

Ben was hyperventilating.

Someone—or something*—is coming...*

CHAPTER 26 *Anomaly*

"Please let it be Mesmo, please let it be Mesmo," Ben found himself muttering over-and-over.

He knew they were coming—the beings from the spaceships. Yet Ben remained rooted to the spot, too terrified to move.

Shadows passed before a crackled glass window in the wall separating his room from the corridor. And before he could react, they were there, standing in the doorway.

THE TOREQ!

Five of them, tall and intimidating. White hair, sleek bodies, blue-grey one-piece suits, honey-coloured eyes. Two women: one with short hair, the other with an asymmetrical side-bob; and three men: one with hair plastered backwards, the other two with a short, single braid running down their back.

All five with their eyes on Ben.

Ben forgot to breathe.

The short-haired woman entered, lifted her glowing hand, and scanned Ben from where she stood. A tingling sensation like pins-and-needles travelled through his body, then was gone.

The alien woman pulled back.

"Well?" One of the alien men spoke.

The woman's eyes narrowed as she stared at Ben. *"The readings are clear. It is this A'hmun child who is emitting the signal. It is weak now, but undeniable."*

The hairs on the back of Ben's neck rose. *Jeepers! I can understand every word they're saying!*

Now all eyes were back on Ben, and he wished the ground would swallow him whole. With a few long strides, they were in the room, surrounding him.

The plastered-hair man spoke to him with disdain. *"You have stolen a Toreq skill. Why?"*

Stolen? Ben's mind went blank. His voice had evaporated. He was still struggling to recover from the initial shock of being surrounded by alien beings—aliens who were not Mesmo. *The*

Toreq! These are Toreq aliens, standing right before me!

The woman with the side-bob frowned at Ben. *"He does not understand. Give him a translation device."*

The plastered-hair man lifted his hand, a small, black button-like object balancing on his fingertip. But the short-haired woman grasped his wrist before he could place the object behind Ben's ear.

"Wait!" she said, eyes widening. She scanned Ben with her glowing hand, sending another wave of pins-and-needles through his body. *"He does not need it. The A'hmun child is already using the translation skill."*

More staring.

Crap! It was as if they could see right through him!

Now the plastered-hair man's voice turned to ice. *"Why do you possess a Toreq skill?"*

Ben opened his mouth, but nothing came out. He wanted to blast passed these beings who were not supposed to be here—not supposed to be here *at all*.

"Answer the question!" The humanoid snapped.

Panic surged through Ben in waves. Where

did he get his skill? *Think!* "Kaia!" he blurted—
Kaia, Mesmo's daughter. The original owner of
the skill. The alien girl who had died after
transferring the skill to him.

The plastered-hair man straightened and
glanced at the others. Their heads turned to one
another as if exchanging a silent message. *"The
Observer did not mention that his daughter's skill
had survived,"* the humanoid said. His nose curled
as he glanced back at Ben with hard eyes. *"You
disgust me, thief!"*

Ben flinched.

Wait! Did they really think he'd *stolen* the
skill from Kaia? *And the Observer... the Observer...*
Ben's mind whirled. *They're talking about
Mesmo!*

"Ask-k M...m...esmo..." Ben mumbled. He
shut his eyes in desperation. He was so terrified he
could barely get the words out of his mouth.

The woman with the side-bob reached out a
finger and touched the blister on his mouth. A
warm sensation seeped into his lip.

"Stop that!" The plastered-hair man barked.
*"We do not heal A'hmun scum. Definitely not a
thief like this one."*

"Hey!" Ben objected. *A'hmun scum... Thief...
Is he done insulting me already?*

The woman pulled back and spoke to her companion. *"The A'hmun child has information on Mesmo. The wound was slowing his speech. We won't get anything out of him if he cannot speak."*

Ben licked his lips. The blister was gone.

"Fine. We will discuss this more once we are back at base. We have delayed long enough," the plastered-hair alien said.

At base? Ben's mind flipped, the words darting around in his head. What base? Why, and where did the Toreq have a base?

His legs turned to jelly. The plastered-hair man caught him under the armpit just before they could give way and pulled him aside.

A strong wind blew behind Ben, sucking him back. He turned and gawked.

One of the braided-hair men had raised his arm and stuck his glowing hand through the window as though it were water. Round ripples formed as the glass disintegrated, leaving a gaping hole that led outside.

Powerful gusts of wind filled the room as the opening widened. Ben's sandals zipped past his face, sucked into nothingness. The bedframe rattled.

Ben felt a strong pull, his feet almost lifting

from the ground as if he were being picked up by a giant vacuum cleaner, but the alien's strong grasp kept him grounded. Then the air stabilized, and Ben realized the other braided-hair alien had his own hand outstretched and sent a tunnel of blue light from inside the room to the spaceship.

Around this unnatural cocoon, furniture shook, the shoe-box fell off the bed and slipped across the floor, then toppled over the edge. Yet, within the crackling filaments emanating from the alien's hands, the air was calm.

"Let's go," the plastered-hair alien said. *"The Challenger is waiting."* And with that, he pulled Ben to the edge of the skyscraper.

No! Ben's mind screamed, teetering an inch from certain death. Hundreds of feet of empty sky spread before him. He must have been hundreds of floors up, in one of Dubai's tallest skyscrapers— and they wanted to pull him off the ledge!

The short-haired woman sighed, exasperated. *"The A'hmun does not understand,"* she said, pushing past him and stepping on to thin air. Blue filaments crackled under her feet as if she were stepping onto an invisible bridge. With a few strides, she had crossed the void and entered the spaceship.

The side-bob woman followed.

Ben's captor pulled him by the arm again.

Ben resisted, spots swimming before his eyes from terror. Another hand grabbed his other arm. With a single step, Ben was whisked from the floor and carried out into the open.

Ben shut his eyes, heart leaping to his throat. He'd tumble to his death for sure, meeting a terrible end on the concrete far below.

But nothing happened.

Instead, his feet landed on something soft, like rubber. He risked a look down and found his feet stepping on air, blue filaments indicating where he was in contact with the unnatural bridge. The earth spread far, far below, making his head sway and almost causing him to faint. But with an alien on either side, holding him, they crossed the gap and were inside the spaceship in a heartbeat.

Ben blinked at the gloom that met his eyes. He noted hovering screens, Toreq men and women bustling about, the city of Dubai spreading out before him through a wide window.

A tall Toreq straightened and turned to them. His white hair was combed back and attached in a thin, waist-length braid. His small, honey-coloured eyes were hard and his cheekbones, pronounced. He looked much older than the others.

Ben guessed he must be some sort of Captain or General because a certain air of authority hung around him. Or maybe it was the impression he gave because of the cape that fell down his back to his feet.

"Challenger," the plastered-hair alien spoke to the tall leader. *"We have found the source of the anomaly."*

Anomaly? Is that what Ben was now? An anomaly? He tried to call forth the skill, so he could attempt to speak Toreq, but his mind was too rattled for it to obey. "Mesmo!" he breathed in despair, speaking in English. "Mesmo will be here any minute!"

He'll explain. He'll set things right!

"Mesmo..." the tall alien repeated thoughtfully. Did his eyes soften? He blinked and, the softness was gone. "I am General Zoltar, also known as the Challenger," he said, startling Ben because he spoke English. "Who are you?"

"B-Ben A-Archer..."

Zoltar studied Ben for a long time.

Ben did not like it. It was as if Zoltar was staring straight inside him, judging his skill, judging *him...* A direct glance sent shivers up Ben's spine. There was a gleam there. A calculating, scheming, *displeased* gleam.

"Challenger," the plastered-hair alien interrupted. *"This A'hmun scum possesses the translation skill. He says he stole it from Kaia."*

"No, I didn't..."

"He is the cause of the anomaly," the short-haired woman cut him off, speaking to Zoltar.

What anomaly? "No, wait..." Ben began, but the ice-cold look that Zoltar cast his way told him nothing he said would convince him otherwise. The alien's mind about his guilt was already made up.

Ben's heart dropped like a stone. "But, I... I didn't..."

Zoltar's voice burst loud and clear. *"Let this be yet another sign of A'hmun treachery,"* he spoke to his Toreq crew. *"Let the A'hmun child be a symbol of his people's downfall and a reminder of why we cast our enemy far away from us, banishing them to this forsaken rock."* He paused, then straightened. *"Initiate operations. Our duty calls. Let us make the Arch Council proud."*

He shot a glance Ben's way. "And if the Observer still lives, then he will know where to find us."

And with that, Zoltar faced the front of the spaceship, which hurtled past the skyscrapers and beyond, and Ben realized with agonizing certainty that he would not see home again for a very long time.

CHAPTER 27 *Downward Spiral*

Blurred light. Jumbled sounds that didn't make sense. Mesmo blinked.

Now that Einar had removed the communication damper from the spaceship, streams of information gushed from the spacecraft's computers. They contained messages. Toreq messages. His people were calling to him from the depths of space. Over and over, they informed him that they were sending scouts to Earth from the warships in a last attempt to find him. They needed to locate him soon.

"Attack is imminent." the message said.

A movement nearby startled him.

The Toreq woman who had knocked him out was standing by the door, checking a device.

There was a shuffling sound outside the spaceship, and Einar heaved himself on board. Grunting, he leaned against the wall, his face black with soot. His eyes fell on Mesmo and filled with hate. *"Why is he still alive?"* he complained.

"Maybe because you let him get away," the woman seethed. *"Focus now. Is it done?"*

Einar nodded, lips pressed together.

"Good," she said, struggling to fix something on the device.

Mesmo groaned, still feeling the effects of the blow she had given him, and he knew she must be skilled in electricity or air, or some other Toreq ability. He tried to stand but found his hands bound to a pipe running through the base of the spaceship.

Einar and the Toreq woman stared at him.

She handed the device to Einar. *"Here. Make yourself useful,"* she said.

Einar took the object from her, still glaring at Mesmo.

The woman stepped forward. She wore the cape of a high-ranking official over her Toreq outfit. Her long, white hair reached her hips, and her face belonged to a middle-aged woman who exerted command. She lifted her left hand and placed her three middle fingers to her front in a customary gesture of greeting. She may have had Mesmo at her mercy, but she still respected his rank.

"I am Captain Daria. You find yourself in a precarious situation, Observer," she said.

Behind her, Einar snorted.

The woman lifted an eyebrow but said nothing.

"Only because you have decided to make it so," Mesmo said. He couldn't take his eyes off the information that was streaming through the spaceship's computers. All this time, the Toreq had been in the Solar System, trying to contact him, trying to warn him of their imminent attack, and he had not seen them coming.

"Release me," he said. *"You already know I am the Observer, appointed by the Arch Council themselves. As a Captain, you are then also aware that my rank supersedes yours."*

"Once, perhaps," she said. *"I was there, the day you were appointed Observer. I admired you for taking on such a noble mission. But that mission is long over. The Arch Council has sent us to eliminate the A'hmun. It is a clear and direct order. There is no turning back. And anything that stands in our way must be eliminated."* She paused. *"You can imagine how disappointed I was*

when I learned of your treason, Observer."

"You lie," Mesmo said, ignoring her accusation. "The Council would never make such a drastic decision without my feedback and that of the seven Wise Ones. Since you seem so well informed, I trust you are aware that I never sent the seven keys to the Council."

Something snapped loose from the device Einar was trying to fix. The Norseman had pressed too hard on it, hearing Mesmo's words. He shot a deathly look Mesmo's way.

Captain Daria pursed her lips and crossed her arms. When she spoke, her voice was low. "As I said, acts of treason..."

Einar fixed the device and straightened, "It's done!" he growled. "This would be a good time for your crew to pick us up, Captain."

Captain Daria nodded. "They are already in position, waiting for us." She laid cold eyes on Mesmo. "Don't take this the hard way, Observer. This is war. There can only be one winner, and you have chosen the wrong side."

Mesmo struggled. "I won't accept such a random judgment from a Captain! I want to speak to your General!"

Captain Daria unfolded her arms and stepped away, ignoring him.

Einar sniggered under his breath. *"The General would like that, wouldn't he?"*

"Shut up, Einar!" Captain Daria snapped.

Mesmo stared. What did that mean? *"I demand to speak to the General, whoever he may be!"* he insisted. *"The law demands you obey my request! Does the General even know that I'm alive?"*

The woman yanked the device out of Einar's hands, shooting him an accusing look, but didn't respond.

Mesmo stopped struggling. *"He doesn't, does he? You are acting on your own! Who is the one who is committing treason now?"* he yelled.

Captain Daria paused, snowflakes entering the spaceship and swirling around her white hair. Her voice was grave. *"There are two-hundred-thousand of us on those warships, Observer. Two-hundred-thousand noble and courageous Toreq who forfeited a life on the Mother Planet in order to wage war against the A'hmun. We are willing to sacrifice ourselves to save our people's future. We will see this done, no matter the cost."*

"War? What war?" Mesmo burst. *"This will be a massacre!"*

Einar had bent down to pick up something from the floor. He flipped open Mesmo's smartphone and smiled, then turned the screen around so Mesmo could see it. *"Well, well. How about that?"*

Mesmo froze, remembering he had asked Laura to send him a message with Ben's location.

"It looks like your little protégé has reappeared..."

Captain Daria waved a dismissive hand at Einar. *"Forget that. I heard the news. The A'hmun child was picked up five minutes ago."*

Ben! Mesmo tensed. *"If you so much as touch him...!"* He roared, struggling to break free.

Einar threw the phone at his feet. *"Oh, don't worry. I'll be sure to send him your regards."* He sneered and followed Captain Daria out of the spaceship and onto the mountain-side.

Mesmo roared again and pulled frantically at the bonds. His eyes fell on the phone's screen. It indicated a backwards count.

0:59... 0:58... 0:57...

"Are you sure this will erase all trace of the spaceship?" Mesmo heard Captain Daria ask.

"Relax," Einar replied as the door began to close. *"I know what I'm doing. The volcano will take care of everything. We'd better get off this island."*

Dread grasping his stomach, Mesmo yanked

unsuccessfully at the bonds. His eyes fell on the backpack Laura had given him before he had left to recover his spaceship. He reached for the strap with his foot, pulled it towards him, then struggled to unzip the top with his teeth. Breathing hard, he found it, the reusable water bottle she had packed for him. He tipped the backpack so the contents would slip towards his back. Grimacing, he stretched one hand and painstakingly inched the bottle out, then unscrewed the top.

0:17... 0:16... 0:15...

Water poured out of the bottle onto his wrists, but he almost lost his chance when his skill wouldn't come forth. He clenched his teeth and pulled at the humid ropes, the skill reacting in sparks, but finally heating the bonds to a sizzling point that split them.

0:04... 0:03... 0:02

He freed one hand...

0:01...

...desperately pulled at the other.

0:00...

A deafening blast. Shockwaves rattled his bones. Hovering screens flickered and died, the Toreq messages disappearing forever.

Mesmo freed his other hand.

The spaceship tipped. Another set of

explosions. Terrible, agonizing sounds came from below, and the ground ripped apart before him through the spaceship window. A deep gash appeared in the mountain, and black smoke billowed from the entrails of the Earth. Metal screaming against rock.

Mesmo grabbed on.

The spaceship teetered, then tumbled towards the lava below.

EPILOGUE

The skyscraper glimmered in the bright afternoon, its blue-grey windows reflecting the sharp rays of the sun.

A handful of tourists who had been admiring the tallest building now stared at the mysterious blue lights that hovered in formation around the 109th floor. Their videos would circle the world multiple times thanks to social media, spurting on thousands of comments from believers in alien life, conspiracy theorists and scornful naysayers. Mostly, though, they attracted viewers who said the images stirred feelings of curiosity and wonder.

The three UFOs hovered with surprising ease around the skyscraper, then rose higher and higher towards the tip of the tower that pointed like a gigantic futuristic needle towards the Moon. Two other UFOs that had been stationed in the sky to the right and left of the Dubai skyscraper flew in their direction and circled them as if in a dance.

Then, in the blink of an eye, all five were gone, having reached supersonic speeds, causing onlookers to gasp. Tourists zoomed their cameras in on the top of the tower, searching for the UFOs, yet only finding the Moon that became ever larger on their shaky screen as hands struggled to hold still.

Had it been possible to observe the far side of the Moon, perhaps humans would have had the smallest warning of things to come.

For, behind Earth's rocky satellite, five monstrous spaceships, similar in size to the Dubai skyscraper, hid in the darkness, waiting.

Metallic voices murmured between the alien craft—preparing, calculating, devising. For in the clash between the different alien species, there could only be one survivor. There could only be one victor in the *Second War of The Kins*.

THE ADVENTURE CONTINUES:

Ben Archer and the Toreq Son
(The Alien Skill Series, Book 6)

www.amazon.com/dp/B08HWQYPH5

LEAVE A REVIEW:

If you enjoyed this book, please leave a review in the 'Write a customer review' section:

www.amazon.com/dp/1989605176

PREQUEL:

Read the prequel to The Alien Skill Series,
The Great War of the Kins:

www.raeknightly.com

The Alien Skill Series continues!

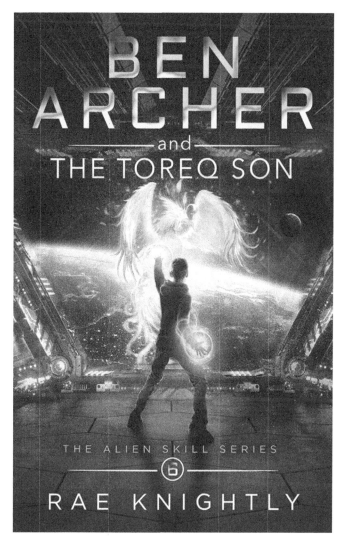

Turn the page and start reading...

CHAPTER 1 *New York City*

An unprecedented downpour battered the City of New York. Citizens hunkered in their homes, trying to sleep in spite of the drumming rain, wondering how they would get to work the next morning while they soothed their frightened children. Lightning and thunder struck, rattling windows and briefly illuminating a sky as black as swirling coffee.

Secretary-General Adhira Prabhakar stared out the window of her 32nd floor office, listening to the deluge rather than seeing it, because she had placed her glasses on her desk and everything looked blurry.

She sighed and took a file off a pile of documents. It was one of a dozen urgent reports that had come in in the past week, with unnerving reports of sudden, catastrophic droughts in Central Africa, abnormal flooding in Europe and a gargantuan hurricane heading for the Gulf of Mexico.

The head of the United Nations placed her glasses over her nose again and opened the file.

Sirens blared within the building. Startled, her pen slipped out of her hand and dropped to the floor.

A soldier erupted into her office. "Code red!" he barked. "Ma'am! Follow me, please!"

Adhira jumped to her feet.

Code red!

Something major was happening. Code red meant imminent danger. Get to safety first, then ask questions.

In a calm manner, she rushed to a safe, pressed a code to open it, and pulled out highly classified documents that needed to stay by her side at all costs.

"Ma'am!" the soldier repeated, the urgency in his voice palpable.

Adhira would not succumb to panic. She ignored the soldier and finished what she was doing.

The documents now safe in a briefcase, she

headed out of her office without addressing a word to the soldier. There was no time for chit-chat.

Her heart skipped a beat when she glimpsed soldiers rushing to the windows, aiming their weapons outside. She gritted her teeth but didn't stall and headed for the emergency stairs.

Procedure required her to head to the roof, where a helicopter would be waiting. A soldier barred her path and said "Downstairs, Ma'am!"

She faltered a fraction of a second.

Plan B, then.

'Downstairs' meant she was headed for the Emergency Operations Bunker located deep below the United Nations headquarters.

The threat was closer than she'd expected.

What could be impeding her from leaving the building skyward? It couldn't be the storm, could it?

Flanked by soldiers in front and behind her, she started the long decent, secretly thanking the stars that she was still in good shape despite her advanced years. Her morning jogs, which she had continued to practice even after being appointed Secretary-General two years ago, came as a blessing in this precise moment of urgency.

A Sergeant joined them on the 12th floor.

"Secretary General," he said in manner of greeting, falling in step behind her.

"Talk to me," she said.

"Ma'am, an unidentified craft has landed on the Garden Court. It's some kind of stealth craft. It doesn't show up on any radars. Security observed it on visual alone. The US military is sending in F-16 fighter planes. They are waiting for word that you are safe before they engage to destroy."

"Engage to destroy?" Adhira started. "How long has this craft been there?"

The Sergeant glanced at his watch. "An estimated nine minutes and twelve seconds."

Adhira slowed down, forcing the other soldiers to do the same. "If this craft were hostile it would have attacked long ago, don't you think?"

The Sergeant shifted nervously. "Ma'am, we'll figure that out once you're in the Bunker."

They started down the stairs again, Adhira deep in thought. "It doesn't make sense. Why are they here? Who are they? Terrorists? For goodness sake! A secret US operative? Who?"

This time it was the Sergeant who slowed down. She saw him gulp. "None of them, Ma'am."

He turned to head down, but she held him back, her eyes full of questions. He wouldn't meet her gaze, but he said, almost apologetically, "We determined the craft's trajectory. It..." he cleared his throat. "...it came from space."

She let go of his arm, staring at him.

"It is an unidentified flying object," he said, his voice thick. "We don't know who it belongs to or what it is, but one thing is certain. It is not from Earth, Ma'am."

By now everyone stood still on the stairs.

Not from Earth...

"Are you pulling my leg, Sergeant?"

He blinked rapidly, sweat pearling his forehead. "I have seen it myself, ma'am. I am not pulling your leg."

Adhira felt an almost tangible ripple of fear wash over them. She continued her descent in silence, weighed down by the news. Thoughts crashed in her head, as she tried to grasp the facts without giving in to panic.

By now they had reached the fifth floor.

Before anyone could react, Adhira reached the exit door and barged through it into the open office space.

"Ma'am!" the Sergeant shouted in warning behind her.

"I need to see for myself," she said without turning around.

Soldiers spilled into the area after her.

"Ma'am!" the Sergeant repeated, catching up with her.

She ignored him and strode purposefully towards the northern windows overlooking the Garden Court and East River. She glanced around and grabbed binoculars from a soldier standing nearest to her, then aimed them out the window.

"Ma'am! We need to go!" the Sergeant barked, but she knew he wouldn't dare drag her away by force.

She aimed the binoculars at the garden and saw it.

The craft. The unidentified flying object. The words flashed in her mind like a warning.

It was larger than she had expected, sleek and dark. *Hovering...* She adjusted the binoculars. Yes, the UFO seemed to be floating on thin air. A helicopter whizzed by, its floodlight piercing the torrential rains, and Adhira was surprised to detect a thin filter of blue light around the craft, as if it were stationed within a bubble.

The lack of a sign of life from the UFO made her skin crawl, because it was clear this celestial object had not landed here on its own.

Who—or what—piloted it?

A commotion made her turn.

A pale soldier ran up to her and saluted.

"Secretary General," he said, out of breath, holding up a wireless red phone. "The President of the United States."

She had already recognized the phone. She grasped it and held it up to her ear, staring through the binoculars again. "Mr. President," she said.

"Secretary-General," the deep voice said. "Are you safe?"

"I'm looking at the intruding craft as we speak," she said.

"Adhira!" the President scolded. "This is not a drill. I don't know who they are or where they came from. If they don't identify themselves within the next minute, I'm sending in the F-16s to destroy them. We can't afford to wait until they decide to attack the UN or New York."

"Peter," she said, also addressing the President by his first name. "I'm informed that this unidentified craft is an *alien* spaceship. As in: *not from this planet*. I don't have time for jokes. Are you confirming this information?"

There was a pause on the other end, then the President said, "I am."

Adhira pursed her lips, pushing down waves of wonder and fear. "Peter," she said into the phone. "Hold off the strike."

"What...?"

She hung up and handed the phone back to the soldier. "Sergeant," she said. "You may get yourself and your men to safety—if you wish. I'm going to stay. Whoever is in that craft landed at the foot of the United Nations headquarters for a reason. This is not a random decision. If they had destructive intentions, they would have acted minutes ago, and we wouldn't be standing here staring at it." She shook her head, determined. "No, if we are indeed looking at an extraterrestrial vessel, then I won't be labelled as the one who turned down humanity's first peaceful contact."

"Target in sight!" a soldier shouted.

"Take position!" the Sergeant barked, thrusting his own binoculars before his eyes.

Adhira did the same.

An opening appeared in the spacecraft, spilling light from inside onto the lawn. A single form filled the doorway, then stepped out onto the grass and walked some ways away from the craft to the edge of the bluish bubble.

Security must have finished installing floodlights, because they switched on, suddenly bathing the Garden Court in bright, white light.

Adhira leaned forward, squinting. She gasped. "Wait a minute! Is that...?" she began.

The Sergeant—voice astounded—finished the sentence for her. "...a *boy*?"

Continue reading:
Ben Archer and the Toreq Son
(The Alien Skill Series, Book 6)
www.amazon.com/dp/B08HWQYPH5

About the Author

Rae Knightly invites the young reader on a journey into the imagination, where science fiction and fantasy blend into the real world. Young heroes are taken on gripping adventures full of discovery and story twists.

Rae Knightly lives in Vancouver with her husband and two children. The breathtaking landscapes of British Columbia have inspired her to write The Alien Skill Series.

Follow Rae Knightly on social media:
Facebook/Instagram/Twitter/Pinterest
E-mail: raeknightly@gmail.com

Acknowledgments

To Deema Kheiry, Zer Zabar, Mahtab Narsimhan
for invaluable cultural feedback.
To D'artagnan, Robin, Mystee, Giselle, John for
your continual support.

To you, reader, for taking the time to read
Ben Archer and the Star Rider.

Thank you!
Rae Knightly

Made in the USA
Las Vegas, NV
28 February 2022

44782615R00163